THE DIG

The Dig

Cynan Jones

COFFEE HOUSE PRESS

MINNEAPOLIS

2015

First published in the United States by Coffee House Press, 2015

Copyright © Cynan Jones, 2015

Originally published in English by Granta Books under the title *The Dig,* copyright © Cynan Jones, 2014

First published in Great Britain by Granta Books, 2014

A version of one chapter of this novel was originally published in *Granta* magazine in 2012

Excerpts from *The Long Dry* and *Everything I Found on the Beach* copublished in Great Britain by Granta Books and Parthian Books, 2014. First published in Great Britain by Parthian Books.

Cover design by Murray & Sorrell FUEL

Typeset in Vendome by Lindsay Nash

Author photo by Alice Fiorilli

Coffee House Press books are available to the trade through our primary distributor, Consortium Book Sales & Distribution, cbsd.com or (800) 283-3572. For personal orders, catalogs, or other information, write to: info@coffeehousepress.org.

Coffee House Press is a nonprofit literary publishing house. Support from private foundations, corporate giving programs, government programs, and generous individuals helps make the publication of our books possible.

We gratefully acknowledge their support in detail in the back of this book.

LIBRARY OF CONGRESS CATALOGING-IN-PUBLICATION DATA
Jones, Cynan, 1975-
The dig / Cynan Jones.
pages ; cm
ISBN 978-1-56689-393-0 (softcover)
1. Animal welfare—Fiction. 2. Rural conditions—Wales—Fiction.
3. Psychological fiction.
I. Title.
PR6110.O624D54 2015
823'.92–dc23
2014039064
PRINTED IN THE UNITED STATES
FIRST EDITION
FIRST PRINTING

This edition for Colin and Metz.

HE PULLED THE van into the gateway and dropped the lights. It was a flat night and the van looked a strange, alien color under it. For a while he sat there carefully.

It was lambing time and here and there across the shallow valley and variously on the hills there were lights on. And while it looked to him from this distance like some community at work, he knew that all those farms were involved in their own private processes, processes in their nature give or take the same, but in each space of light carried out in isolated private intimacy.

He looked out across the scape and recalled in those wells of light those farms which were sympathetic or against this thing he did. In his time he had covered most of this ground and in his mind he drew vaguely the shape of the lands that attached to each farm and called back the names of each property he knew as if he were noting constellations.

It was a time of mixed certainty for him, with these people awake at night; but they were also busier and distracted, and with that general busyness disregarded noises more readily, accepted them as products of another's work. Attributed more readily the distant bark of dogs.

He was a gruff and big man and when he got from the van it lifted and relaxed like a child relieved of the momentary fear of being hit. Where he went he brought a sense of harmfulness and it was as if this was known even by the inanimate things about him. They feared him somehow.

He opened the back of the van and the wire inside the window clattered and he reached for the sack and dropped the badger out. He spat into the dirty tarmac beside it.

The dogs had pulled the front of its face off and its nose hung loose and bloodied, hanging from a sock of skin. It hung off the badger like a separate animal.

Ag, he thought. The crows will sort that.

He kicked the badger round a little to unstiffen it. He kicked the head out so it lay exposed across the road. Its top lip was in a snarl and looked exaggerated and some of the teeth were smashed above the lower jaw, hanging and loose where they had broken it with a spade to give the dogs a chance.

They hadn't had the ground to dig a pit so they had fastened the badger to a tree to let the lurchers at it and its hind leg was skinned and deeply wire-cut.

That could be a problem, he thought. That could be a giveaway, but everything else is fine. The other injuries would be disguised.

The badger's underbelly was torn and ripped where they had let the terriers at it before he had finished it off with a shovel.

Messie was good tonight, he thought. She was good and persistent.

The badger's teats were pronounced and swollen with feeding and several of them were torn off and the pelt was slick with the mix of blood and milk.

It's a shame we didn't get them cubs, he thought.

He thought about tearing off the leg.

Ag, I wouldn't get it, he thought. I wouldn't get that off. He was suddenly repulsed by the idea of touching the badger again. Of giving it any reverence.

The idea of hiding this act suddenly made the big man angry and fatigued. He had been up all night and the walk and the hard digging and adrenaline made him tired, though it came up only as a swelling of anger in him.

He got back in the van and it sagged under his weight. He took off the gloves and threw them into the passenger seat that was bearded with dog hairs. A little way down the road he turned round and came back and drove over the badger. Then he turned round and did it again.

He let the van idle and got out and stood over the sow. The skull was smashed to remnant. He looked at the leg and it still stood out like butchery unnatural and premeditated.

Bitch, he said; then he ground his foot down on the leg, and stamped over and over, smashing the thin precise line of the wire out of the raw flesh.

PART ONE

The Horse

chapter one

———

THE DOG STIRRED as Daniel came between the buildings and got up in its chain and stretched and yawned and in the torchlight Daniel saw this lazy stretch and the torch-light caught on the links of the chain.

He went through the feeding yard, the cattle crunching at the feed ring in the spilled-over floodlight from the shed, and he heard the dog shake and settle again in the kennel behind him.

The night rippled with stillness.

He went into the sheep shed. The ewes were variously rested and the place was maternal and quiet. There was just crunching, the odd cough of sheep. He rested the torch on the shelf and turned on the light and some of the lambs bleated and there was a clatter from the warming box as the orphans excited at the thought of food.

While he waits for the kettle to boil he walks the shed. From the beams hang compact discs, strange astral things in this half-light, now ignored by the sparrows and starlings they are there to keep out. Every now and then they catch some light with some incongruous Christmasness and he thinks of her hanging them, her other things of quick invention, as if she were a child making models off the television.

A singular moth flutters in through the wind baffles to the naked bulb above the kettle, cuspid, a drifting piece of loose ash on the white filament, paper burnt up, caught in the rising current from some fire unseen, unfelt.

At the back pen, one ewe pads the ground, her lip lifting like a horse mouth. It is his shift, he must stay until she lambs, though he knows this Beulah breed are good mothers and often need no help. He knows she is close, that it will not be long.

The kettle rolls mechanically, steam bowling into the light of the bulb, and clicks and he makes the mix and while he rests the wide jug to cool on the shelf he checks the stalls, the tired lambs somnolent and pliant under their mothers' warmth, and lifts out the water buckets, cupping out the floated hay and the droppings that stain chromatographical in the water; and the thunder of filling the water buckets at the tap does not disturb the soft crunching of the slumbered ewes, lying as if exhausted after eating, a thing replete about them. And in this quiet night he feels briefly, as if something unseen touches his face, the ancientness of this thing he does, that he could be a man of any age.

He looks again at the ewe, padding, and goes to her and she grinds her teeth and looks goat eyed at him and he sees the lamb presented backwards, the small catkin of tail tadpole-like in the sack, the obscene bag proffered from her vulva glistening with dark water.

He puts the ewe on her side and puts the gel on his hand, its bright pink surgicalness foreign in its manufacture against this natural process. There is an understood geography, familiar and mammal, as if some far back thing guides his hands about the lamb inside her, understands the building of the baby, this thing he does, which could be repellent, comfortable to him somehow, the warmth, the balloon warm and lipid. It is only visually there is shame. The fluids and motherly efforts are beyond that, too ancient for shame, and he understands a great and vital force at work, equanimical with his instinct, and assured.

He pushes back the breaching lamb, its mother prone, fallen in crunching straw, teeth crunching. He looks nowhere, working with gentle strength, thinking, far away, unfocused. There is a brief sound of rain. Quiet crunching. The light rain on the tin above, and outside the suck and clap of cows feeding in the floodlights. And the rain goes quickly. A hiss. The hiss of the water troughs filling.

He finds the back legs, cups the sharp hoof in his palm as he folds each back and draws it somewhat from the ewe; the throb, power of pelvic girdle and birth muscles chew his arm. And then he draws the lamb in one smooth strong stroke, and slaps and rakes its wet mosslike fur to make it breathe, feels the power of its fast heartbeat in the chicken-bone cage of its ribs, still wet in his hands from the grease of birth, all these things of life, from jissom to mucus slavered between thighs to the wet sack of birth and glistening oiled newborn thing—all of these things of life awatered.

He looks about himself, trapped between the trough and hurdle, sees the plywood starling be-shitted at the stop-end of the trough, the immediacy of the smell of hay, which in his mind can only smell of hay for he has no reference to any other thing. He is almost crazily tired, craves her help, for some company here mainly, to help the effort on. But this is now the rhythm, the way the shifts will work. He feels as if his body runs only on the air in it, but he knows, feeling even as he is, a feeling of strength—of a reserve of strength; like he could give more, whether tired or not, that this thing is of purpose utmost.

He lets the mother clean the lamb, tea-dipped on birth and tannin colored, and as she nibbles at the covering bag he works the fat clotted cream globule of first plug from her stiff and giving teat, this vital colostrum come.

He leans from the ewe, stares down and there sees a head of barleycorn, vertebral and desiccated amongst the straw like a skeleton in a bird pellet.

He rests on his knees like that, a man ancient in some aspect of prayer. He feels oaken and finds once more vapors of energy with which to lift him and, somehow, dazed, he gets to his feet once more, goes about the work, the brief rain passed, outside the sucking and clapping of the cattle feeding in the lights.

For a while he stays and watches the Beulah get to its feet. It is straight up, its instinct to live, head held high quickly, its gray-and-black-spattered coat in still loose rolls; it is vital with instant curiosity, an interest in air, even in its own feet.

He bends and drinks from the tap, can taste the plastic of the pipes that bring the water in, hears even in her absence the rebuff, how she brought refilled bottles of fresh water to the shed, albeit from the same supply, from their kitchen tap.

He thinks of her sleeping now, the rest she needs, thinks of the warmth of her body, the nest-like thing she could be to his tiredness. Then he notes the new lamb in the book, writes in the backward presentation, flicks back and traces his hand across her writing, looks up to the tub of dropper bottles and sprays he does not understand, that are her domain, like the movement records, and the paperwork, all the more careful aspects of the farm.

He watches the Beulah on its feet, its interest in the air, and watches it take its first few steps.

He stood and looked out, understood the strange ventriloquy of sounds that disturbed his land; how a barking fox could sound as if it were right the other side of the farm, how in this prehensile night there could come the illusion of the sea nearby. He listened to that, still as it seemed: the wind coming over the trees then dropping through the hedges and over the fields with the distant noise of waves breaking and running. And such was its likeness that he could not be sure this wasn't the sound of the shifting tides carried from the coast that was dropped away out of sight a few miles off.

He looked up at the bare ash branches, mercurial and somehow elephantine, rising out through the low floodlights and they hardly stirred, making the sound seem very far away. A distant white noise. A noise bearing some primitive hushed whisper of the permanence of vast things.

The sound seemed tangible in the air, and everything felt silent before it. The sheep sighed and crunched, the cattle's feet slapped as they moved in the mud. The dog chain rattled like coins in some dark pocket. But this sound brought stillness.

As he looked out in the pitch dark beyond, a barn owl came into the floodlight, glid silently between the barns and was gone, seeming to leave some ghost of itself, some measureless whiteness in the air.

He went into the boot shed and clicked the light and took off the old jacket, patched with blood and vital fluid, the inner arms birthmarked with shit, floured with grassdust that stuck to the lanolin which through all the embraces had enoiled the coat. He took off the hat. He lifted down the waterproofs over the top of his boots and stepped out of the boots on to the cold concrete floor and pulled his trousers out of his socks. For the brief second he stood balanced on one leg he knew he was stupefyingly tired. Even this small act was almost too much.

He lifted the boots out of the doorway and set them next to hers. His boots looked protective somehow. Her boots and trousers looked smaller next to his, the two pairs like an adult crossing the road with a kid.

He stepped into his shoes without putting them on properly and went to the house. The backs of the shoes were so long crushed that they had molded by now to his heels.

For most of their life the shoes had gone only the ten yards or so from the porch to the boot shed, or perhaps now and then to the log store a little way beyond. The uppers were unscathed and the soles were hardly worn but the backs of the shoes were crushed into a rag. At first they looked comfortable and loved, but actually they had the unfulfilled imbalance of things that had not been used to their fullness. The one part constantly abused had given up and, while the rest of the shoes held up, the wear of doing just one repeated thing had made them useless for any greater purpose.

He felt the doorjamb under his hand and rubbed the worn wood there as he kicked his shoes off. He had long had this need to put his hand upon things—to feel them, as if they were points of reference. The doorjamb, the rough stone on the corner of the porch, the old slate windowsill on the way out to the sheds.

He felt again the way the jamb had worn under his hand, and thought of her. He wondered if there were parts of her like that.

He put the torch on to charge and went into the house.

He looked at the clock. He seemed to notice for the first time it had Roman numerals, though he understood he must have known this. But for a while it fascinated and disturbed him, his new registry of this.

He put on the kettle. He leant against the kitchen unit holding the old beige mug in his hand. He had a sudden strange sense of time—not as a thing you live within, but as an element you grow alien to when you become aware of it, the way you lose the sense of your body being yours when you look too long in a mirror.

I'll give it four hours, he thought, attritionally.

He undressed quietly. He could see where she slept, knew she was unwakeable now. For a long while he had sat at the table holding the tea and when he had finally gone to drink it, it had gone cold.

There was just the light from the landing coming in and in the dark he could almost trace the outline of her in the bed.

The scent of her was in the room and it almost choked him to understand how vital to him this was; how he could never understand her need for his own smell, could not even understand how she could find it on him under the animal smells, the carbolic, the tractor oil and bales and all the things he could pick out on his own hands. He had this idea of smells layering themselves over him, like paint on a stone wall, and again he had this sense of extraordinary resilient tiredness. He wondered what isolated, essential smell she found on him, knew the mammalian power of this from the way pups would stumble blindly to their mother's teat, the way a ewe would butt a lamb that wasn't hers. In the shock of birthing, all that first recognition would be in that smell. They would take the skin sometimes of a dead lamb and tie it on an orphan like a coat in the hope that the mother who had lost her lamb would accept and raise it as her own.

My smell must be underneath everything, he thought, it must be very deep. I don't think it is in the air like hers seems, so it is enough to be around her, you can just walk into it and have the chemical sense of her. She has to come close in to get mine. The way you can only get the smell of some things when you touch them. Even when she is asleep she comes nosing in and it's like she breathes me in and seems to change and settle on me. I don't understand how a woman can like the hard, angular body of a man.

He made soft fists of his hands, stretching the weariness in them. I wonder if she feels from me the thing I feel about her when I touch her. Not in sex, which he understood now was a different thing from everything else. I just mean when I touch her skin before we sleep and I understand all the things beneath it. Animals can't have that. They can't hold their loved ones that way and feel right through their skin. That's never worn off, whatever else. He looked at where she slept. I can't imagine living without that.

He went into the bathroom and did his teeth and realized in his stupefying tiredness that he would never get to sleep in the bed so he went quietly back into the bedroom and took the clock downstairs and sat numbly on the sofa. The fire was burning out. He knew he should keep it in but he was just too numb. He sat with his elbows on his knees and held the clock and listened to the pinging and ticking of the stove cooling, the last settling embers shifting down through the grate, the metronomic ticking of the clock. Three hours. He didn't even want the television on. He stared at its vacant, dark cataract.

They had been through much together, being with animals. Working as a team was a thing in itself most couples do not face constantly, but given working with animals, the small pressures were insistent and regular.

She seemed to suffer more under the smaller problems than the larger, and it always surprised him when she drew on wells of strength to face the bigger crises.

They had both grown up on farms and knew what to expect, but often it was the modernization which wearied them. The paperwork and cataloging and form filling their parents had never had to face, and which confused and sometimes swamped them. Every time an animal was moved it had to be noted, a vaccination given they had to record it. It made sense, perhaps, on the big wide farms the other side of the border, with their managers and offices and employees. But the weight of paper was crippling to a small farm, and neither of them was built for it, so it was a great burden.

They wondered constantly how to improve the return on the farm, thought wildly of turning the outbuildings into accommodation for holidaymakers. But the idea of having these people come into their lives for weeks at a time, of clean, expensive cars on the yard, a ruddy, loud-voiced family all in pristine country gear. He had nothing against these people but they were different and it was impossible to imagine them here, at least yet.

They thought about going organic, but by the time they looked into it with conviction organic lamb was fetching only a fraction more than nonorganic, despite the finalized organic products selling for far more in the supermarkets. The stress and extra controls were not worth it. So they resolved to follow the principles they believed in and ignore the rest, and sold what they could locally through the slaughterhouse.

They looked into direct sales, into doing the butchery themselves, but a licensed vet had to be present when you

slaughtered an animal and their fees for this were prohibi-
tive and the cost of setting up a hygienic place for the
butchery was out of reach; ultimately, the animals had
to go through the slaughterhouse, and they were at the
mercy of the market price.

Sales of the fleeces worked at a loss, the shearers and trans-
port coming to more than the check for the wool; rearing
the stock cattle more or less covered its costs. He thought
of running a shoot on the farm, but the landscape wasn't
challenging enough on one level or expansive enough
on another to bring in the rich guns. They thought of
specializing in rare breeds, of working to giants, even of
alternative livestock like buffalo, or vicuña, whose fleeces
were selling for hundreds. But ultimately, in their bones,
they were sheep farmers, both of them, and they had
gone into it knowing they would never be anything else.
They had buried themselves in each other and the small,
modest, ticking-over thing they had created, and that was
enough while they could manage it.

He could not see this now, through the blur of the work.
He could see it now only as a machine that he had to
keep running, or it would seize up, and he was throwing
himself at it relentlessly as if he were no more conscious
than a part of the device.

I'll miss a watch, he thought. She won't know this one
time. It's quieter now. We've done the glut and it was
quieter tonight, just the one lamb. He accepted the facts

he put to himself. I have to be okay for a while longer so I'll miss just this one. She needn't know.

He blindly set the alarm for eight o'clock, drunk with tiredness. For a moment he thought he could feel the clock ticking, as if he felt right through it. The lamb's heart beating in his hands. Her body under his touch. It's time and touch, he thought. It's these two things. It's because we are aware of them. The draw to go upstairs and climb in next to her warm body was unbearable, but he knew he would not do it. He thought of the way he could feel right through her skin. I wonder if that's why we get so desperate in everything. It's like we're touching something we weren't ever meant to feel.

He put the clock down on the table and lay down on the sofa and pulled the spare duvet around himself. It was the longest they had been apart. She had gone once before for ten days to help when her father had been ill but this was the only other time and he could not accept that it was permanent and that it was three weeks since she'd died.

She went down to the horse to check on it and curry it and in her head there was a strange wistfulness that she did not have a horse of her own and had not ridden for years.

It was a beautiful day, but cold, one of those false starts of spring.

They were looking after the horse for a friend who was having a rough time and going through a divorce and had nowhere to paddock the horse and the horse had just arrived and had hardly made a dent in grazing the field.

The horse was a placid horse but horses are great, instinctive animals and the mare seemed to have sensed the disquiet in her owner and was recently uncharacteristic.

It was towards sundown but there was an hour of light left, especially on such a clear day, and when she got into the field the horse was watering at the pond.

Most horses locally were cobs, but this was a hunter and was higher and more gymnastic.

She walked to the horse, calling it, and began to pat its flank and the horse shook the water from its head and walked up from the pond with her.

Beyond the pond, over the trees, the rooks were circling into a ministry and she watched them as they called and circled and she curried the horse. The horse seemed annoyed and took a few steps away and she followed it but stopped and looked for a while at the farm a few hundred yards off and thought of what was inside her. She felt a great feeling of wealth and happiness go richly and simply through her. And then the horse kicked her.

That was her. She had no thought, and was just dimly aware of the world shutting off before her.

Her brain was dead by the time he got to her and really it was just her body systematically following that he watched.

He carried her the four hundred yards to the house but then turned and laid her down in the barn. He thought she would be furious if he brought her bleeding into the house.

When the doctor came, her head was hemorrhaged into aubergine. The hoof had struck her with the force of a bowling ball traveling at eighty miles per hour and the right side of her cranium was crushed. An x-ray would have looked like broken plasterboard.

The old doctor persuaded him to come in to the house and they waited for the ambulance to come and take her body. He had known them both since they were children and had no small amount of grief and anger at this and they sat with a hopeless passivity at the thing which had happened.

The old doctor was at his desk when he received the coroner's report a few days after. It said in empty scientific language how the hoof had fractured the skull casing and killed the brain. It also said at the bottom of the page that routine tests revealed that she was pregnant. The doctor fought with this information over and over.

He did not know that she had felt this change inside herself, as if she had felt this collision of genes and was sure she knew, had there with the horse that afternoon looked back at the farm and felt this impossible love for it and for her husband and the great rightness of it. He doesn't need to know it now, she had decided, not with lambing coming up. I don't need to test yet. I know. I am sure of it. But I will wait. He will get protective when he knows. Afterwards is better. And she felt girlish with the warm secret of it.

After the funeral in the little church above the farm the doctor carried this information, fighting hard not to just expel the poisonous knowledge of it. As a man of science he had long lived with a solid reverence to the facts. That they were unemotive objects that had to be navigated, as physical as debris in the road. To view them as this was the only way he could tell someone of cancer, of a blood clot near the brain, of infertility. Facts had to out. And so he went to Daniel with this information and with a need to get it from himself.

The doctor was in the living room with the older people and went through and found Daniel in the kitchen where most of the others were gathered. That soft magnetism of kitchens. He looked at Daniel. He saw a solidity and stubbornness in the man that worried him. There was a look something like wildness, as if he was in some long suspended moment of anger waiting to decide on what to bring it down. All this the old doctor saw with futility.

He doesn't need to know, he thought. He doesn't need to carry this. What good would it do?

The old doctor backed away from Daniel, and stood blankly and stared at his paper plate and squashed up the crumbs of sponge with his forefingers and swallowed them with the horrible fact back down.

It's better that he doesn't know. Why would he need that knowledge?

chapter two

THERE HAD BEEN a shattering of rain on the roof of the
dog shed but it had passed quickly. It was not yet light.
Through the door and out through the run the big man
could see inland the darkness beginning to thin and go
powdery, but the darkness still had body, a closed-ness to
it with the passing rain.

The dogs messed around, tumbling over each other as he
took the feed bowls. Only Messie stood still and aloof,
giving just the odd snap at the other dogs if they played
into her space.

The big man looked at her with a kind of reverence,
standing off the other dogs. This dominance came off
her that was difficult to understand in a relatively small
animal like that and he was very pleased of having bred
the dog. Since they took them after his arrest he'd had to
start from scratch.

He poured the dog biscuits that were like colorful chips
of wood into the silver feed bowls and the other dogs
rushed in around him. And Messie just trotted to one of

the bowls and the dogs there made way for her. It wasn't an aggressive thing she did. It was just natural dominance.

He poured a little of the boiled water into the mash and mixed it round and the steam roiled into the light of the single bare bulb that lit up the shed. Around the walls, too high for the dogs, he'd put up the last rats they'd caught. A single nail was through each skull and they hung as misshaped macabre pouches from the beam below the roof as if some giant shrike had its larder there.

He put down the bowl of mash and looked once more at the dog Messie. The man in his big coat was like some puffed-up bird. Ag, you're a special one, he thought. Then he sloshed the leftover water through the door into the run and watched it carry a dog shit away with it in the fog of steam it made across the concrete.

———

Daniel had woken late and for a while lain there almost
stupefied. His whole body felt beaten for a moment, as
if his muscles were made of plaster, the way they could
feel after the first day of haymaking, with the fatigue
of some heavy and unusual sport. Only the mild repri-
mand he allowed himself for missing a shift drove him
up, and once he was up he fell into the automaticness of
it again.

He had been in a way reluctant to go to the shed for
fear of facing some catastrophe being on the other shift
would have averted. A lamb strangled in its own cord; a
young ewe—her pelvis too narrow—prone and sloughing
blood through inside tears, her lamb drowned in its own
bag, the strange hernia of bag split and bulbing from the
uterus, the dead lamb's head magnified in the fluid of its
failed birth. All these things he had readied himself for
as he put on his boots, went to the shed. But all was well.
There was a tiny new lamb just shakily on its feet and
still greasy where its mother had licked it clean. He took
the lamb and sprayed the umbilical stalk with iodine and
made sure the ewe had milk, and then he sprayed the
number on the lamb and the ewe.

The wind soughed through the baffle netting of the shed
and every now and then threw a fine rain against the corrugated tin that pinged and tinkered and brought somehow a
greater sense of warmth within the shed. Briefly, there were

gapes of sunshine through the fast-shifting clouds, but they came and went like laughter provoked in a crying child.

He did the automatic thing of changing the water buckets and checking the pens and then he mustered energy and cleaned out the stalls, feeling his body loosen under the work and every now and then looked over to the newborn lamb to see that it was drinking.

He reached in to the empty stall with the rake, let it bite, and then rolled in the trampled, dirtied bedding which moved as a wad, like some foul turf. Those stalls that had not been occupied for long were fine, and the bed came up lighter and more haphazard, some of the dung witnessable as solid objects in the straw. But those that had longer occupation were variously filthy and had a silage heaviness. Some smelt Marmitey, others had the smell of piss and illness. He was convinced he could sense illness in the air in some medieval way and trusted this even in relation to his own body and his personal understanding of his health. I am just tired, he said to himself now, I am not ill. I would sense it, and I am not.

As the wind soughed through the baffles he felt the cords in his arms loosen, casting out the rake then grubbing in the wet straw and forking it over the pen into the barrow until the act became compulsive and he determined to take up every piece of loosened straw off the dark stony ground beneath.

He clicked on the kettle and wheeled the barrow out of the shed and took it to the heap and tipped on the rotting bedding. Around the field crows were turning over the dung and taking up the worms. They made a strange black contrast to the fresh white lambs. Even in their adjutant walking they contrasted.

He stood holding the barrow. The hedges were not yet beginning to green up. It was as if there was a holding back to them. The ewes cried ritually and the lambs bleated back and now and then came in from play and pushed roughly at their mothers, their tails frenzied as they drank, and here and there were lambs sleeping in their mothers' lee, folded up and catlike.

He went back in and made up the mix and fed the orphans under the warm lamp, noticing freshly as he did every time the tight, carpety compactness of the lambs' fleeces, the way in places the skin was loose with the potential for growth, the force with which they sucked and drank.

The ground of the stalls had dried a little and he filled the spray with water and hypochlorite and pumped it up to pressure and sprayed the floor and walls of the stall, the hypochlorite stinging his nose with the smell of swimming pools.

It was the swimming pool of junior school he always thought of, how they did not talk to each other back

then even though at weekends they played together on
one farm or the other, his farm or her grandparents'.

Then they went to different schools. Her to the Welsh
school when they moved up, and he to the comprehen-
sive in the other town. It was years before he saw her
again. When he did he recognized her instantly. He knew
then. They both knew.

He swilled his cup and swung the leftovers from his cup
under the gate into the gathering puddles and the cloudy
dregs steamed on the mud.

He reboiled the kettle and blew the inevitable flakes of hay
from the cup and made a coffee and poured in sugar from
the bag that was fawn-stained and lumpy. He shook in the
milk mix, watched the powder fatten like wet flour and
sink into the cup, leaving the coffee a strange vegetal color.

Presently it began to rain and within minutes he heard
the rain butt outside trackle with the falling water. He
could go in to the house now, but he did not want to.

Spits of rain came over the gate, making a damp crescent
stain on the ground inside the entrance to the shed. She
had wanted that fixed, he thought. She was right. The shed
faced the weather that came in from the northwest and it
would have made a difference to fashion up some baffle
netting or something to block that wide draught, the rain

petering in. He felt dismayed at all the things he hadn't done, the things he had not fixed. He thought about whether he had wasted time and could have done these things but could not think of when he had wasted time; then he tried to think of everything he did that kept him so busy and there were very few big things he could find, just the everyday running of things. Somehow time had gone too fast. It just goes too fast, he said within himself.

He sat on the bales and let his eyes go round the shed. The sheep shifted into new comforts under the rain but there was nothing doing. The new lamb was drinking. He wondered what sort of a mother she would have made. They had talked about it, were ready for it. He pushed the thought away.

The cat scuttled in out of the weather and rubbed itself on the bales then went into the corner and settled itself and he felt a quiet transfer of love for the cat. His eyes filled with tears. He looked at the cat and held back the tears and felt himself smile desperately. Oh God, he said. You were so good. It was so good to have you.

The cat came up and sat with him, and for a while they sat like that, in the comfortable sound of the rain, and the closeness of the cat was almost too much.

———

The big man got the terriers in the van and seeing the brutalized chainsaw they were cooperative with each other and calmer, different from when they sensed they were working a badger, when they got individual and competitive.

When he got to the farm the farmer came out to meet him. He wore a stiff waxed jacket that looked new and unweathered. He had a seniority to him, a type of important mantle.

This was one of the bigger farms locally and had years ago been one of the manor farms that worked under the big house. You could tell the historical management of it by the wide fields and the way the big oaks were spread out in them.

It was misty here lower in the valley and the oaks looked veiled and there was a chattering of starlings on the wet ground. You could not see most of the birds. It was the sort of open drifting mist that played with the distance of things. You could hear the tractors working somewhere on the land.

There's two spots, said the farmer. He was a magistrate and knew of the man from the hunts. His jaw was sagged from a cynical habit. It gave him the air of being above everything.

The big man nodded and got out the brutalized chainsaw and began to fill it with fuel. He was gruff and taciturn. He had added too much oil to the two-stroke so that the fuel would smoke.

The blade of the chainsaw had been taken off and he'd fixed a rubber pipe to the exhaust. It looked a strange, bastardized thing.

The magistrate farmer took the man over to the big modern barn. After the damp outside air there was a dustiness in the outbuilding.

The man brought the terriers down with him two to a lead and stationed them about the straw bales. Then he started the chainsaw there on the ground.

The noise filled out.

A little straw blew about the floor from the vent of the motor and the big man picked up the saw and revved it, crashing the noise in the barn. The mist had been deadening the noises so it was a very abrupt sound.

The dogs stood stock still, shaking a little with alertness, their eyes shifting minutely with little rapid surveillances.

He revved the saw again until it started to choke smoke through the thick rubber pipe. Then with a strange mobility he went round the stack and pumped in the smoke to the gaps and runs in the bales.

When the rats came out they came out with pace but the terriers ripped into them. The dogs were catlike in their speed. When they caught a rat they shook it like they were trying to break its back, which they were. They were yelping. Bites seemed to just drive them on.

The noise in the barn was terrible and solid. There was the clatter of the chainsaw and the metallic yelps of the dogs. That made a main terrible noise. It was a brief, flurried clatter of killing.

When they were done the men lined up the rats and counted them. The big man took the rats that were not quite dead, trod on their scaly tails and systematically smashed their heads with an electric fencing spike he'd picked up from the wall of the barn.

The farmer sickened a little at that brutalism. The dogs were whining and sniffed and their breathing came now in quick loud little pants. You could not smell the straw through the petrol smell and the choked-out smoke drifted about the barn like the mist outside.

There's the log pile too, said the farmer. There was a strange hum in his ears after the noise in the barn. He had a disgust now for the big man but understood him as an instrument. He was surprised and impressed that the man could manage such a discipline in his dogs.

There's something else too, said the magistrate farmer. His jaw sagged with the habit as he looked at the big man. The big man was experimentally putting weight down on a rat under his foot as if he was testing to burst it.

I can have a look, said the man.

Badgers, said the magistrate farmer.

———

Daniel took up the cooled milk mix and took up the black lamb from the warming box. Its head swayed almost imperceptibly with exhaustion. It was like a very old thing asleep.

The earlier wind had dropped and the rain now settled and gathered into a thickening mist.

He husbanded the lamb, heard the brief interior gurgle as he fed the tube down and it met the lamb's stomach. It was a remote sound, like something far off, not there right in his hands.

As the tube reached the lamb's stomach there was a brief smell of its insides, then he fed down the milk. The tiny lamb seemed will-less, its eyes just tired. It was as if they did not have in them any witnessable want for life.

The thickening mist gave an enclosure to the shed. Every now and then the lamb choked back the milk and he fed it with an invasive passivity. He compared this to the willful sucking of the other lambs at the bottle, the way their bellies swelled drumlike. Sounds, outside, seemed to become isolated, lost things.

He heard now the far-off sound of chainsaws. That sound had been constant here with the clearance work they had begun earlier in the year.

It was such a day, he thought back, perhaps the mist thicker, more enclosed. They had stripped the hedges and taken out the gorse and willow by the roots and what was not worth keeping as firewood was put to burn in the field. The chainsaws worked restlessly.

For days from the wet fires dirty smoke shifted up amongst the mist, giving it a rusted color. The fires were gray and mudded where the ash had cooled in the rain but a great heat was still in them and stumps and the bigger branches stood from the slake partially blackened.

The hedges took on a damaged look. They took most of the trees out and he began to resent it. It was taking on what he considered an Englishness, a forced tidiness and management that he did not like. He felt that his closeness to it was threatened because it had visibly changed so severely and because of an intervention by other people. That it had turned into a thing he didn't know intimately any more. It was a visual shock. Like the one time she came home with her hair cut short. They had applied to a scheme to reclaim some of the wasted land and the decisions were being made by the grant people as to what now happened to his land. It was all better in the long run, they said.

He rhythmically pulled the tube from the lamb and it coughed and choked weakly. In a way he knew it stood no chance, but at the same time knew there were no certainties of that kind. Even the weakest thing could make it. Sometimes it simply seemed some element of surprise that carried an animal through.

He watched the motes of mist snaking. Since her death he had asked them to stop the work. There was an aftermath. The field looked battle shocked, the ground stark, an altered sense of light. He couldn't see the fields from the house and he was glad of that. The stumps left in the hedgerows and the sharply angled butts of hazel were bleached and obvious still. It was accusatory, something about it. The fires had not burned down completely and needed to be relit. Already there was a strong clarity in the ditches, a reapplied squareness to the field.

They were ditching. The mini-digger worked in the mist, ship-like in it. Its engine sound seemed flattened. The big pipes to put in the gateways lay about in piles and every now and then seemed to appear in the mist. It was like a dockyard.

The ground of the field was disrupted from the caterpillar tracks of the digger and strongly patterned into zip shapes and the reeds had been crushed and spread beneath them. It looked trodden over. There was a noise, too, to the alteration of the ground.

THE DIG

When they came to the shard the driver let the digger idle and got out and tried to shake it and test it. It wouldn't move. It stood there three feet or so out of the ground at the edge of the field. It was cast iron and had a cooked, hardened look. The shard curved slightly, striated with fine lines as if it had been lathed. The outside face was polished where the sheep over the years had rubbed against it and wisps of old wool hung within the curve.

The driver got both hands on the shard and hefted it but the shard did not shift. There was no flexibility in it.

You won't, Daniel said. He was feeling a disappointment and betrayal that the shard had to come out of the ground. He had mythologized it as a child, a piece of lightning solidified there, a great sword, had over the years battled to move it himself. He thought it the gut of some truck or implement long abandoned and it was like a mark for him. Like the mole she was self-conscious of above her hip. It felt wrong to remove it. It was right in the line of the ditch and it had to come out but he was disagreeing emotionally with what they were doing.

He was not a superstitious man but that is different from building superstitions of your own. He was unsettled at the shard coming out of the ground, as if it would bring a wrongness.

They used the digger arm to push and pull the shard back and forth like a tooth and eventually it loosened a little and the earth made wet lips where it went into the ground.

The digger cleared the earth around and then dug at it and when it came out it came with a wrenched sucking sound as if tearing a bone from a socket. The noise of the two great iron things coming together had been more of stone than metal, the echo deadening in the mist, but when they dragged the shard away from its place the teeth of the bucket skidded over it with a screech. It lay graunched, seven or eight feet long, like a felled tree. Where it had been in the ground it was darker and more permanent looking and did not have the same rusted look. It looked like a knife with a handle.

The men on the chainsaws had stopped to witness the removing and there was speculation as to what it was.

It's a bit of old waste pipe, said one. Drainage. They used to use metal.

Daniel looked at it. There was a wrongness and a loss to it being out of the ground.

It was then the man arrived. He just appeared out of the mist which seemed to emphasize the size of him. He had two terriers with him that went immediately and sniffed about the fires.

Big work, he said. The men stopped and were looking at him. He looked around them all and at Daniel.

Do you want anything rid of? he asked. He looked over at the dragged-up shard. I'm taking scrap.

*No, said Daniel. I don't need it. He knew of the big man.
Knew of his reputation. He had an immediate anger that the
man had come onto his land.*

*Them old implements? asked the man. There was a kind of
unnerving thing to him, there in the mist. It was as if he had
no idea of right ownership.*

*The dogs were yelping in and out of the reeds. He shouted at
them and they quieted. It was a bizarre obedience.*

*No, said Daniel. Part of the scheme was that the rubbish and
scrap, the old implements and machinery had to be got rid of.
It unnerved him, the man coming with this timing. He was
angered but knew he could not provoke the man or give him
reason to feel personally aggrieved.*

*Nothing else? asked the man. There was a load to the question.
A physical weight.*

*The other men were standing around. The big man had
brought unease to everyone. Daniel could feel the mist slightly
on his face.*

No, he said.

•

*When the man had gone Daniel felt a tide of adrenaline. As
if he had been left a threat. The old implements were the*

other side of the sheep barn. It gave Daniel a fear that some-
thing of his had been coveted. He could not disassociate the
man coming from the moving of the shard. As if it had con-
jured him.

He thought of the shard, lying there, a snapped bone.
Something stricken. He wondered briefly again what it
was. It worried him that there was no imagination in him.
There was just a hollow, dead unknowing. Somewhere
within him, the anger about the man coming onto his land.

He listened to the chainsaws he thought were from
the manor farm at the base of the valley and heard the
yapping of dogs, their strange sharp note. An adrenaline
came up in him again. He had a sudden fear for her, a
belief someone had touched her or was going to touch
her and harm her again. It was inexplicable.

———

The big man stood at the entrance to the sett and stared as if he were following the tunnels along, assessing it.

He saw the heap of freshly scuffed soil and the drawn-out bedding outside the entrance. The sett was on a slope and looked to head deep in and there was much undergrowth and thin sycamore on the cover.

I'd need somebody else, he thought.

He went out a little from the entrance and found the dung pit that in the colder weather was often close to the sett this time of year. The fresh spores looked soft and muddy. In the mud around were scrapings and footprints and from their impress he knew it was a big full-grown boar. A sow would put up a better fight if she had cubs to defend, but there was something more competitive to the size of a big forty-pound boar.

On the nearby trees were the unhealed scars where the badgers had cleaned their claws and rubbed off the dirt from their coats.

That's them, he thought. They're here.

•

He followed the river back up from the woods and periodically took out a snare from his knapsack and laid it along the bank.

The water levels had dropped in the last month and the river was fringed with marsh marigold and he set the snares amongst it.

The mink were here now, annihilating the streams and watercourses. It was as well to be able to produce one if they were stopped. It was legal to hunt them, and it would explain the dogs.

When the big man got home he kenneled and fed the terriers and dressed the rat bites then went inside and made the calls.

He talked briefly and arranged that he would call if he got the badger. They wanted something heavy preferably, a real fighter. They wanted a spectacle. Then he called the other man whom he had worked with on the hunts and whom he knew had a good, big dog. He would need a big dog against the possibility of the boar.

It's just a catch and release, the big man told him.

Can I bring my son? the man asked.

chapter three

WHEN DANIEL CAME out of the shed his mother was there. He had not heard her arrive. She had come through the cows and carried the basket that was always on her elbow with the tea towel over it. She had aged quickly some years ago and then seemed to stop and looked now like she had for years. His father had changed differently. He had seemed to be always the same but then went old very suddenly, as if he had given in under a weight.

The basket on his mother's arm gave Daniel a strange sort of locus; he could rarely remember her coming without it. She looked him over, was sensible enough not to judge him in the clothes he was in, and they walked back to the house.

"How's Dad?" he asked.

"Still slow with things," she said. The stroke had split him down one side like lightning hitting an old tree. "He's angry for you," she said.

Daniel nodded.

They went into the house. By the time he had taken off his boots and waterproofs and come into the kitchen she was cleaning up and the kettle was boiling. He felt a slight filial guilt.

He went over to the sink and cleaned his hands under the crashing hot water, a meringue of suds lifting out of the filling bowl. His mother emptied the basket of things, putting out a box of stew, a bara brith. A handful of small rolls.

"Do you want this loaf?" she asked.

"I've got the bread machine," he said. They had bought that together. It was a thing of wonder to them. There was no false politeness.

"You're not eating."

There was nothing to clear. Just the scuffs of butter and crumbs off the plates some toast had been on, the odd bowl of cereal. A tinned pie was his one effort at hot food, and there was evidence of the tin.

She dumped the plates into the suds and made the tea. For years this had been her kitchen, the center of the place where most of the important things of her life had happened.

"Stew's easy," she said as she put down the tea. She knew she had to be careful with her son. "Dad sent you these," she said.

She handed over a carrier bag of *Farmers Weeklys*, back issues his father had already read. He could see where his father had thumbed and bent the pages. He still subscribed to the magazine and, like most farmers, was more shrewd and politicized than you would think. That the carrier bag was already on the kitchen unit made it clear his mother had already been in the house but he didn't mind. Even in his head it was still his parents' farm, though the idea of ownership and of the possession of it occurred to him only obtusely. He had grown up here and belonged to it and it was not like some property external to him. He felt more possessive over his tractor.

He understood how it must have been difficult for his wife to come into the place, but she did so gently, without displacing anything. The bigger changes they seemed to make together, putting the shower in, painting the upstairs rooms. The house took her in just as the family had. She had come to play as a child and then there had been a long ten-year gap, but it was as if the house remembered her and accepted her in the way a dog might recall an old friend of its owner.

"How is it?" asked his mother.

"Steady," he said. He began to tell her the counts and the small crises and the surprises and they talked for a while, the conversation shifting about like something in the wind being lifted and dropped, left for a while, lifted again.

His mother had a staid, farmhouse traditionalism. You could go abroad to an agricultural place and you would find the same taciturn dependability in the women there. You would be able to sit at their table and there would be the same ironic hospitality, and then they would unload cookery at you and you wouldn't be able to move. If you were hurt, their responses would be nurse-like and unsympathetic but their remedies would work, and if you were to make one of them angry it would be a great and dangerous thing. They are like this because they have been charged for generations with keeping their men working, by feeding and repairing them, and there is no room for sentimentalism in that. You would not find kinder people, but their kindness would be in essential things and they would pour it on you.

But this sureness of purpose can only come from having a defined role and from not questioning it. It was certain to him that his mother had never questioned the role, but with that same conviction—age being a role in itself— she had adopted oldness when she assumed she should, rather than when her body told her to.

She had seemed to prematurely age, to adopt some strange outwardly witnessed notion of old people in the way

teenagers put on some adulthood. There was no adjust-
ment to the fact that eighty was not a rare age anymore,
and that sixty was what forty used to be. She started to
order elasticated trousers and strange shoes that made her
look incongruously aged like teenagers look in grown-up
clothes, and seemed to choose a stock phrase book of senior
comments which she took to saying with a wistful acceptance; again, like a teenager trying to sound grown up.

He didn't know exactly what to do about this, but it was
wearing. And then suddenly she was old, and the incon-
gruity was not there.

Like a teenager finally growing up and letting the honest
little bits of character from childhood come through, now
his mother actually was old there was something once
again more girlish to her, and he could trace this. It was
as if he was coming to know her as the person she was
before she even had him. There were all these little signs,
and he began to understand how there must have existed
a great chemistry between his young parents that had
gradually been rhythmically buried by life. The role, he
thought, looking at her now, understanding her fearful-
ness at having to split her care once more between her
husband and son, his father half-paralyzed and he bereft.
It's the role, he thought. The role gets you through.

"Ma," he said. "I'm okay. I don't want you to come round."

"It would tire two people to death, this," she said. He saw in her eyes the flash at the word she'd spilled, saw it catch in the air before her and shifted his head, letting her know she could let it go. She understood that he was not being proud, remembered his childish independence and hoped it would be enough.

"I have to get through this," he said. "It's easier if I don't see anyone. I have to just get through. It doesn't matter how I am."

He tried to put it as clearly as he understood it. He could not bear the responsibility of small talk, of reassuring people he was coping. He seemed to know the offer of sympathy would be like a gate he'd go crashing through. He could bear only the huge responsibility to the ewes, to the farm working, which would be tyrannical and which was in process now, and which didn't care about him.

"After?" asked his mother.

"I don't know after," he said. And truly he didn't. She held him then, and she felt the massive devastation of him.

PART TWO

The Dig

chapter one

————

THE BOY HAD not slept. He was gawky and awkward and
had not grown into himself yet. When his father came
to rouse him he found the boy awake with expectation.
Warm, remember, said his father.

The boy nodded loosely in the way he had. The way was
to have a minute hesitation before doing things. This
came from trying to be eager and cautious at the same
time around his father.

He was long and thin and he could have looked languid
without this nervousness but instead he looked under-
developed. When he got out of bed in his T-shirt and
shorts it emphasized the awkward gangliness of him. He
had the selection of muscles teenage boys' bodies either
grow or don't but the skin on his face was a child's.

He got dressed and went downstairs. In the kitchen he
sat at the table with the kind of extra-awakeness not sleeping can give you and started automatically to spread paste
onto the sliced bread. He had a low-level excitement
running through him. A day off school. He felt the same
illicit closeness to his father as he did when they went

lamping and in these times he was capable of forgetting that his father did other things.

His father put the tea on the table and filled the big flask and then they sat and blew on the tea and drank it. Then they went out.

They took the dogs from the run and got them in the car and drove off the estate. The boy found the smell of the sawdust and dog shit in the run hard to bear in the early morning. The smell of it was a strange note against the deodorant he enveloped himself with.

He had not been digging before and was trying to imagine it. He imagined it frenzied and was excited by this. He did not know it would be steady, unexciting procedural work and that it would not be like ratting at all. He had broken his own dog to rats himself and this gave him pride. When they picked on him in school he kept his pride in this. He hung on to it.

The boy's father parked the car and they sat seeing the dog runs and the broken machinery and the boy was momentarily stupefied by the darkness and emptiness about the place. In the car lights he could see just beyond the runs the bodies of cars like some disassembled ghost train littering the field.

The big man heard them pull up outside and saw the car lights catch and reflect on the mesh of the run and came out to them. The boy had a brief inarticulate awareness that his father shied a little when he saw the big man come from the house. He hadn't seen that in his father before. The boy thought the man looked like some big gypsy.

The man leaned into the window and the dogs in the back came alive at this new presence and set off a yapping, which set off a yapping in the dog sheds beyond. The car was full of a deodoranty smell that got into your mouth.

They yelpers? asked the big gypsy.

They're good dogs, said the boy's father.

It stinks, said the man. It's a girl's bedroom.

The big gypsy looked accusingly at the boy and the boy felt himself redden. He felt the nervous flush go up in his throat.

They're good dogs, said the boy's father.

We can't have them hardmouthed, said the man.

No. They're good dogs, the father said.

We can't work with hardmouthed dogs, the big gypsy said. The big gypsy was looking at the terriers, taking them in. The boy could feel there was a grown-man tension.

Then his father said: They're not hardmouthed, mun. They're good dogs.

There were three terriers in the back. One was the big Patterdale, Jip, thirteen inches at the shoulder and a solid fourteen pounds. He was about as big as you'd want for a badger dig without being too tall in the shoulder to suit the holes. It was why the man had called the boy's father, thinking of the big boar.

What's the pup? said the big gypsy. He nodded at the boy's dog and the boy felt the redness on his throat again.

She's just along, said the boy's father. The big gypsy looked at the pup.

She's not going down, said the big gypsy. He had to take the badger and there was too much risk the young dog would not be able to hold him.

The boy felt this shame and the crushed feeling from school came up in him.

She's just along, the boy's father said.

———

chapter two

THEY PARKED UP in the machine yard of the big farm and got the dogs out and coupled them dog to bitch with the iron couplings.

In the east a powder of light was just coming and in the barn the tractors looked immense and military. At the edges of the fields the trees were still a solid deep black.

They coupled the boy's pup to the older dog and coupled the gypsy's older bitch to the big Patterdale. They had to couple the right dogs. Dogs that could work together at rat could fight at a badger dig, as if they sensed the individuality of the process.

They got the tools and divided them up to carry; then they took the big five-liter tubs of water from the van and the bag with the tin drinking bowls and the food and gave them to the boy. They weighed on him immediately. It was crisply cold and with their thin handles the weight of the water bottles burned on his fingers.

They went through the gate and down the lane, letting the dogs run in front of them, passively aware of which dog took the lead of the other as they rooted in and out of the hedgeside at the dying scents laid down in the night.

Mud had gathered in the track and the overnight rain left it wet and the boy, alert and cold and overawake, took in the sucked sounds underfoot and the clinking of the coupling chains and the body sounds of the dogs as they pushed through the undergrowth of the bank. He was using the gulping sounds of the water sloshing in the tubs as a kind of rhythm to walk by.

The thin light was beginning to increase and the few bean-shaped flowers on the gorse stood out with unnatural luminosity. The men's feet went down hard and solidly in the lane, but the boy constantly tripped on the loose stones the winter's rain had brought down, as if he didn't have enough weight to himself.

They went off the track and whistled the dogs in as they went over a field, the lambs prone and folded next to their mothers. Some of the smaller lambs wore blue poly-thene jackets against the rain and they looked odd in that first light and overprotected.

The boy could hear the ewes crunching and one or two faced the dogs and banged a foreleg on the wet ground, giving a thump that sounded like kicking a ball. He wished he could play, but he was clumsy against the other boys and this inability was just another little cruelty to him. Even now, he looked out across the lightening field and saw himself catch a high kick, the crowd of trees a fringe of spectators. But then—the school field, the ball smashing off his fingers, the laughter of the other kids. That was the reality of him and it brought up a wad of sick and anger.

They worked their way down through the topped reeds that stubbled the slope at the base of the field and stopped by the brook and the boy set the water down. They put the dogs to lead. His pup was shaking a little with excitement.

She's got rats somewhere, he said. The sentence came out on the swell of pride and he realized it was the first time he had talked in front of the man.

The man lifted up a tub of water and unlidded it and took a rough swig.

Keep her in, he said. The bank's snared.

The boy was made thirsty by the river and wanted to drink but he did not like the idea of drinking the water after the big man had drunk from the tub.

In the relative openness of the lane and across the field the dawn light had been enough, but here things closed in and they checked the snares with the torchlight.

Bar the one, the snares were empty. The boy heard the dogs whine with the scent of something and the man signaled them to hold back and the boy put the water tubs down and stretched his fingers. Then the boy heard the dull crack of the mink's skull and for a while did not register what the sound was. The man had hit it with a foldaway spade.

They went on. The water had become convincingly heavy to the boy now. The scrub began to encroach the bank until it was thickened and difficult to pass and after a while they cut away from the stream. It was heavy going but somehow the big man had mobility in it and seemed to fit into the countryside in a way the other two did not.

The dogs sniffed in and out of the torch beams ahead of them and the men pushed through the sprawling holly and they drove into the wood. Every now and then they disturbed something and there was a clatter in the branches or the tearing of undergrowth as something fled. The wood thickened. Everywhere there were branches down and in the strange beams of light some looked animal and prehistoric.

•

They staked the dogs some way from the sett and poured them water and took a drink themselves. The boy had a queer feeling about the man's mouth being on the water and still did not want to drink it.

The trees had opened up a little and you could see the light finally coming through. There was a moment of greater coldness, like a draft through a door, and the boy felt an unnerving, as if something had acknowledged them arriving there. They had made a lot of noise moving through the wood and when they stopped they heard the birdsong and the early loud vibrancy of the place.

First dig? said the man.

The boy nodded, with that hesitancy. They could hear the dogs lapping and drinking at the water bowls.

The main hole's up there. The big man gestured up the slope. We'll put in the dog, he said. He meant Jip, the big Patterdale.

The big man's own bitch was by his feet, with her distant, composed look against the other dogs.

I want to put her in next. He indicated. Better be a dog goes in first. The big man was thinking of the big tracks and the possibility of the big boar. A bigger dog would have more chance up front. They knew if you put a bitch down after a bitch, or a dog down after a dog, there were problems most times; but if you changed the sex the other usually came out with no trouble.

The boy's father nodded agreement. He was checking the locator, checking the box with the handset.

The boy was thirsty and looking at the water, not wanting to open the other tub in front of the man.

Take him round and block up the other holes. I'll do the other side.

The big gypsy brought out the map he'd drawn of the holes and went over it with the boy's father. The gypsy asked the boy if he understood and the redness came to his throat under the zipped-up coat collar; but he was feeling the rich beginning of adrenaline now. He was dry and thirsty and had a big sick hole of adolescent hunger but he could feel his nerves warming at the new thing and began to feel a comradeship of usefulness to the man.

They unwound the sheets of thick plastic and went off and systematically blocked the holes with stones and sheets of plastic and laid blocks across the obvious runs with heavy timber and then went back to the dogs. Then they went up the slope with the two first dogs and gathered around the main entrance and stood the tools up in the ground.

There was old bedding around the hole, the strange skeletal bracken starting to articulate its color in the gray light. Jip started to bounce on the lead and strain for the hole as if he could sense the badgers. The strewn bracken might have meant the badgers had gone overnight, but from the way the dog was behaving there was a fresh, present scent.

The boy looked at the dog straining on the lead and could feel the same feeling in his guts. He felt the feeling he did before the first rats raced out and the dogs went into them.

The boy's father knelt with the excited dog and checked the box and collar over again and Jip let his enthusiasm solidify into a determined, pointed thing and stood stockily facing the hole, a determined tremble going through him.

The boy's father studied the locator once more and checked the signal, then they sent the dog in.

The boy was not expecting the delay of listening for the dog. He could feel his stomach roll though. He could feel a slow soupy excitement. This was a new thing. Then deep in the earth the dog yelped. Then again; and his father was instantly by the hole, prone, calling to the dog, calling with strange excitement into the tunnel.

Stay at him, boy. Good Jip. Good Jippo.

The boy glanced at the man as his father called this out, as if it had revealed what he was thinking about the way the man looked. But the big gypsy seemed to be rapt, a pasty violence setting in his eyes as he listened and watched Messie, his bitch, solidify, focus. Finally, the dog let out a low whimper of desire.

You could hear the barks moving through the ground now and they came alternately sharp and muffled until they seemed to regulate and come with a faraway percussive sound.

The big man moved across the slope. He seemed to swirl in some eddy, then came to a halt, as if caught up on something.

The big man moved again, listening, and the boy's father tracked across with the locator until the two men stood in the same place, confirming the big man's judgment.

Here, he said.

They brought up the tools and they started to dig.

•

It was very early spring and the bluebells were not out but made a thick carpet that looked newly washed and slick after the rain. They cut through this carpet and cleared the mess of thin sycamore from the place and the big gypsy cut a switch and bent it into a sack mouth and laid the sack down by where they would dig.

The ground was sodden with rain and sticky and they worked with the sharp foldaway spades, cutting through the thread roots. The smell of rotted leaves and dug-up soil strengthened. When they came to a thicker root, they let the boy in with the saw. Then they started to dig for real.

The big man swung the pick and the father and boy shoveled. Within minutes the boy was parched with thirst and hunger and could not shout properly when they called constantly to the dog below. He was dizzy with effort. He was afraid of not being able to keep up with the men. As the hole deepened they shored up the sides of the hole with the plastic sheeting and the work steadied to a persistent rhythm.

The badger was going nowhere and it was not about speed but persistence now.

•

After two hours they stopped for a drink and ate some of the paste sandwiches. The big man ate nothing. The dry soil on the boy's hands was tide marked with water from the blisters that had torn and were flaps of skin now and there was a type of dull shock in his back. He had been expecting more action, not this relentless work, and he didn't understand it.

The dog had been down for two hours and had continually been barking and yelping and keeping just out of the badger's reach for that time.

Every so often, the boar rushed the dog and the dog retreated and the badger turned and fled; and Jip went after him through the tunnels and junctions until they reached the stop end.

Then the badger turned and ran at the dog again. It was nearly two and a half times the weight of the terrier and armed with fearsome claws and a bite that would crack the dog if he landed it properly. But the dog was quick and in his own way very dangerous. Jip kept barking. Yelping. The badger faced him down and every now and then turned to try and dig himself into the stop end. But then Jip moved in and bit his hindquarters, and the big boar swung round again in defense.

In the confined tunnel of the sett, the constant yelps were deafening and confusing like bright lights in the brain of the badger and it was unsure what it could do. It was then a standoff. A matter of time.

They sent the bitch in and Jip came up. He looked like he was grinning. His mouth was open and flecked with spit. The dog was exhausted and thirsty but gleamed with the event somehow and when they took off the box and collar, steam came into the morning air off his body. The boy was confused that they ignored the thick obvious blood that came out of the Patterdale and spread down its throat.

The boy kept looking nervously at the exhausted bleeding stubborn dog. The fresh blood seemed a synthetic color against the dun-green slope.

Messie's good, said the big man. She'll hold him for the rest.

The boy sat and held his blistered hands against the cold metal of the foldaway spade. He had gloves but he did not feel he could wear them. Steam rolled off from the plastic-flask cup of tea and it came off the body of the injured dog. Steam came too off the lifted soil, but no birds came as they might to a garden, as if they knew some dark purpose was at work.

The man's bag hung on the tree and the head of the mink protruded. The boy looked at it. The mouth was drawn and the precise teeth showed. He thought of one of his earliest memories, of his father holding a ferret and sewing its lips together so it couldn't gash the rabbits it was sent down to chase. The mink had the same vicious preciseness as the ferrets.

Get your dog on it, the big man said. The boy immediately felt the redness at being talked to.

He nodded.

She on rats?

The boy nodded again. He had a panicky lump in his throat.

Good rat dog should take mink. Start them early.

The boy felt the swell of pride come up and mix strangely with his nervousness.

Nice dog, commented the man.

They'd gone through finally into the roof of the tunnel and it looked now like a broken waste pipe and it was midmorning when they lifted the terrier out. There was still an unnerving composure to her, a kind of distant, complete look.

The boy did not understand the passivity of the badger and that it did not try to bolt or to struggle. He had to develop an idea of hatred for the badger without the help of adrenaline and without the excitement of pace and in the end it was the reluctance and nonengagement of the animal which drew up a disrespect in him. He built his dislike of the badger on this disgust. It was a bullying. It was a tension, not an excitement, and he began to feel a delicious private heartbeat coming. He believed by this point that the badger deserved it.

The big man was in the hole alone now, his shape filling it. The boy's head pumped hotly from the work and finally his nerves sped.

Have a spike ready, his father said.

Then the badger came out. It shuffled, brow down as if it didn't want to be noticed. It sensed them and looked up and the boy looked for a moment into its black eyes, its snout circling. The boy was expecting it to have come out snarling and fighting with rage, but it edged out.

It had been trapped in three or four feet of pipe for hours and it edged out until it was by the opening and the big gypsy took it.

He got it round the neck with the tongs and it struggled and grunted and then the man swung it up and into the sack with this great output of strength. Then it kicked and squealed and you could see the true weight and strength of it and the boy didn't understand why it hadn't fought at first, at the beginning.

The badger scuffed and tried to dig and the big man punched the sack and the badger went still. At this, the boy felt a comradeship with the man again and a sense of victory, holding the iron spike there in readiness, as if he was on hand.

We'll hang him while we fill things in, said the big gypsy, stop him trying to dig.

They filled in the hole. Threw in the old roots and stones they'd dug out and finally put back down the sods of bluebells. The place was slick with mud and trodden down and the ground of the area looked like the coat of a sick dog.

The big gypsy looked at the sack hanging from the tree, at the sack-like weight of it.

It was the second time he'd dug a badger for the gang. That first time, Messie had been just a pup. He thought of the money. It was worth the risk. He made a point now and then of taking in a badger he found genuinely hit on the road to the Veterinary Investigation Center and he carried the receipt slips in the van to produce if he was stopped. But that worked only for dead badgers, or to explain the hairs they might find. He had to move the live badger and it wouldn't matter what else was in the van if they stopped him.

The big man reached into his bag and took out the mink and threw it to the boy. Its damp weight and the limp, sumptuous ropiness of the animal surprised him as he caught it. The mouth was drawn and he could see the precise teeth.

You can keep him, the big man said. They're vermin here. It was like a payment for things.

The boy felt a glow of pride and the sudden warm team-ship with the man that was alien to him and which he had difficulty with. His father looked at him with a strange grin and the redness came to him then.

He lifted the mink's lips to see the needle teeth. They were like sewing needles. He looked at the needle teeth and felt the fur of the rope-like body. The electricity was gone out of it.

Give her a shake tonight. The big man nodded at the pup. Good rat dog be good on mink.

The boy's father was panting and looked brightened. The boy could see the sweat on his father's head through the very short hair. The adrenaline was coming in the boy now and he looked at his pup and swelled with pride. He felt a warm cruelty, standing there on the beach of soil.

I'll start her tonight, he said to himself.

———

When they got back to the yard after taking the badger it was gone midday. The boy was exhausted and tired. The boy had been expecting the same kind of flurry as ratting and he was in shock at the monotonous graft of the dig.

How's the dog? asked the big man.

The boy's father picked up the big Patterdale and looked at his throat and chin. There was a glancing scratch underneath its jaw and a little way back was a tear some two or three inches long that had bled all down the dog's front. The dog seemed unperturbed.

Stitches? asked the gypsy.

Aye, said the boy's father. He lifted the cut flap of skin up, peeling it from its own blood, and holding the dog more firmly as it bridled. The blood had soaked into the rough coat and it was jammy.

There's nothing cut, he said. The dog's artery was a fraction above the cut and he could see it pump thickly through the dog's skin.

The big man had not put the badger down at all and when he put the sack in the back of the van he swore once, succinctly, at the release of weight.

They uncoupled the dogs and let them sort themselves out and the boy watched his pup work over a log pile with the other dogs. They were frantic with the scent of rats the big man had driven out the day before.

The boy was ratty and awkward himself and he watched his pup with a proudness, thinking of the mink the big man had given him. It had given him a teamship with the big gypsy.

What's for him? said the boy's father. He nodded at the sack in the van. Behind the big gypsy the farmland looked wider and tamer without the mist. You could hear the tractors work somewhere again on the land.

I'll take him somewhere, he said.

He divided up the money that the magistrate farmer had given them for getting rid of the badger. He did not mention the other men, nor the five hundred pounds they were paying for the big forty-pound boar.

When the others had gone, he pushed the sack to the back of the van and carried over some straw bales that he put in the back hiding the badger. He thought of leaving the tools and coming separately back for them but then thought, Ag. If they look in the van they'll find it anyway. Just the badger was enough to send him down.

He drove home without incident though and got the dogs from the van and unloaded the bales and took the badger and dumped it in the sack in the coal bunker. Then he went in and called the men. They said they'd be ready for it that night and they gave him a time and directions. It was about three in the afternoon. Ag, he thought. He figured on getting some rest.

PART THREE

The Cloth

chapter one

THE BLACK LAMB looked tired and beaten under the lamp.

It had not put on weight and he could make out the fingers of its ribs with the bloated milk-full stomach behind them. It was folded in the bottom of the box, but not with the folded comfortable way of a sleeping cat, more with the weak compliance of something sick beyond will.

Daniel picked up the small black lamb. His father would have simply dashed its head on the barn floor. He was not a hard man, but a pragmatist; but that kind of will wasn't in Daniel. Despite the lamp the lamb felt cold, as if it could generate no heat of its own, and it was too light for itself and hung limply. It was as if he'd picked a jumper from the floor. It had a completely will-less passivity.

I don't expect this of you, he said. I just want you to understand it. Sometimes you have to choose between a quick misery or a slow misery. He heard his father talking, saw him take the useless lamb from the box. You have to understand it as an option. There was a movement and

the lamb hung dead from his father's hand, a thin spittle
of blood reaming from its mouth.

He heard the voice again. Heard his father, that there
were the two miseries, and somewhere in him a vicious
voice told him that his wife had no fear now of the worse,
drawn-out misery that might have come. Hers had been
the quick misery, the head dashed against the barn floor.
He thought of his father stricken, becalmed by the stroke.
He ignored the vicious little voice, as if it was something
overheard he had no wish to know.

He rubbed the lamb, trying to bring some warmth into
its muscles, the wrinkles of the loose skin riding under
his hand like rolls of sock. There was the superstition that
every flock should have a black lamb to sacrifice should
the Devil come and it was to Daniel like the lamb was a
victim of this.

He felt the lamb's heartbeat under his hands. It was faint.
A bare registry.

You need to live, he thought.

He picked up the lamb and carried it into the house.

He put it down in the porch and took off his boots and
then went in and found a box and came back for the
lamb.

He opened the door of the Aga and took out the racks.
He hadn't cooked in it since she had died. There was just
the residual automatic heat of it running and he took
out the racks with unprotected hands and felt inside the
oven space. Then he put the lamb in the box in the Aga,
leaving the door open, and went back outside.

———

The policeman opened the door, looked at the deep mud of the yard, and got deliberately out.

Set back from the window, the man watched him through the gap in the curtains. He watched him scan the place. The policeman was young and he was not a policeman the big man had seen before.

The policeman bent through the car door and pushed the horn twice.

What do I do here? thought the man. He wished he'd left one of the big dogs off but knew even through the coal it would scent the badger and bother it. If I stay in the house, he'll start looking round, thought the man. Ag.

The policeman had started to walk toward the house from the car and the big man came out.

Afternoon, sir. It's clearing up, the policeman said. The policeman looked at the man and looked out as if at the weather over the valley.

The big man just nodded.

Few questions, really, sir. The policeman was light and inoffensive the way they are and the man moved to bring him away from the house.

Can you tell me what you were doing last night, or early this morning?

The big man didn't reply.

The policeman looked around at the yard and privately noticed the two sets of tire tracks that were cut into the mud and that were not filled with overnight rain. He saw the old red van and guessed one set belonged to that. The policeman took in the many dumped engines and tires and the wastage of vehicles and machines about.

We've had a report of fly-tipping. He waited. I just wanted to ask whether you would know anything about that.

What did they tip? asked the man.

The policeman didn't respond. He was looking at the junk and the big man saw and said, Does it look like I throw things away?

Just wondered if you could help, sir, said the policeman.

Somebody pointed at me, said the man. The two men stood in the yard.

The policeman could sense the man was guilty of something but knew he had not been tipping. He was suddenly aware of his singleness at the place. He knew the man

had past firearms offenses and way back some assault.
He didn't respond to the man, using the silence instead.

I was here last night. Asleep.

The policeman smiled. We had quite some rain, didn't
we. Kept the kids awake, he said. He felt this horrific electricity coming off the man. The policeman was smiling
but he thought briefly and preciously of his kids.

I don't know, I was asleep, said the man.

Did you go out this morning?

I just fed the dogs. That's all.

The policeman looked over to the dog run with distaste.

What sort of dogs do you have? he asked, as if he had an
interest in them.

Some big ones and some little ones, the man said. This
couldn't be it, he was thinking. They were like this when
they raided the house. They had these stupid questions,
then the rest of them all came out from nowhere.

You haven't been out this morning? asked the policeman.

No, said the man. Somewhere in the near distance a chainsaw started up and some of the terriers yapped, knowing the sound from going ratting.

The policeman looked round at the yapping of the dogs. Anyone been here? he asked.

No, said the man.

The policeman thought of the tire tracks without the rain in them.

Mind if I take a look in the van? he asked.

The big man's heart quickened as his brain worked through his routine, as he went over each step. Yes. He'd followed his routine. He nodded at the van and the policeman went over and opened the back and looked in. There were just some palettes and bales in there. The policeman felt this horrible inside apprehension as he turned his back on the man. He had an extreme dislike of him.

Distantly, the chainsaw was biting and idling. It stank of dogs in the van.

The policeman stepped back and smiled at the man and made a kind of "everything's fine" gesture.

Well, he said. Thanks for your cooperation. *Something is wrong here,* he knew. He thought again of the rain keeping his children awake and thought how easily someone like this could turn, and thought again of the firearms charges and how there should have been backup, and he knew there was something wrong with the man.

He looked out over the valley and then at the dog run and then he drove off.

———

When the policeman had gone, the man went to the coal bunker and lifted out the badger. From inside the sack, the badger had dug into the pile of coal and the sack was torn and blackened with filth.

The big man knelt by the bath panel and pushed it and the plastic wraithed against the bath as it flexed and he took hold of the sharp top of the panel and bent it over and lifted it off. Knelt down like that in the big coat, the bulk and actions of the man looked bearlike.

He stood the panel out of the way against a wall and with his face down smelled the dry piss and the unclean-liness around the toilet and the copperiness of the old pipes. He had the kind of extra-awareness of when you see a commonplace thing from a different perspective and noticed the way the copper pipes had the strange eucalypt green on them that looked somehow stony.

Just inside the space under the bath was a row of various pots and dishes filled with sharp-smelling raw detergent that he had put there to curtain any scent the police dogs might find and he moved them to one side. There was something almost comic in the way the big man had to be careful and delicate to do this, to not spill them.

Then he lay on his shoulder in the aspect of some big mechanic and reached under the bathtub and brought out the sack from where it was tucked up the other side.

He unwrapped the gun and looked at it and then he wrapped up the gun again. He put the sack down in the bath and with the awareness saw the dog hairs in the bath and the strange brown stain under the taps from the long time it had not been used.

He put the bath panel back on and took the gun outside and went down to the boundary fence where the machinery was crashed and growing in amongst the trees and then he wrapped the gun in a second plastic sack and put it in amongst the machines as if it was just debris. Somewhere far off he could hear a woodpecker trat on a tree.

Let them come now, he thought to himself. They can search the house.

———

For a moment sunlight had come tipping in through the slats of the barn again but it was gone now and the golden pool with it and Daniel traveled the length of the troughs with armfuls of hay as the ewes hefted round him to feed; and it was then, as he unfolded the hay, that he found her cloth.

It was just a thing she had, like a comfort thing—a bright piece of pink patterned cloth that was variously a hair tie, a headscarf or bandana, or was worn about her neck to stop the dust and grime tracking down her collar. It was as much a thing of her as the Stanley knife she always carried for snipping the bale bindings or a hundred other purposes. It was a difference between them that she always carried a few specific things—her cloth, the uncomplicated Stanley knife, an old strapless wristwatch —to meet the simple repeated questions of their daily processes while he relied on brute strength, guesswork, or the availability of some thing he could make use of. He felt it important that there were solid differences between them, whether, as he knew, she was right in some things or not.

They were haymaking and she was wearing the cloth as a headscarf against the beating heat inside the tractor cab.

They were in the new field at the top which they had acquired that year and that had been historically part of the farm before his parents had sold it off. For a few years it had been grazed by a handful of sheep the hobby farmer put there, and on and off Welsh Cobs had come and gone, cropping the grass to a baize turf. But for a long while the field had been untended and had gone feral.

Over the winter they took off some of the bramble that balled chaotically about the field, and tore up the sentinel blackthorn and gorse that advanced off the hedgerows, burning the cut stuff down into two or three impossibly small piles and there was a childlike enjoyment in the way the various thorn crackled and flamed so ferociously.

Later, they took a scarifier over the grass to scrape out the dead, yellowed stuff and let the new growth come and they let the field become meadow.

In the way things gather names, the field came to be called *cae piws*, the pink field, as cleared of its wild growth it burst into a display of red clover and tufted vetch, with sprawling beds of fumitory. The field then seemed to stick to its scheme as ragged robin appeared and isolated cuckoo flowers, and shyly, in the damper corner a rarity of orchids. Into this they even let the thistles come, their stiff, pinnate leaves turning brittle in the sun as they cut them down before their buzz-cut pink crowns turned to seed.

Naturally, as the months wore on, the grass outgrew the flowers and it was into September before they cut the hay, when she lost the piece of cloth, as if the field had taken back this piece of pinkness into itself in return for what was cut. And there it was, as if she had only just dropped it, stiffened and bleached with hay dust, as if she had left it on the radiator as she always did and it had slipped quietly down.

For a while he could not touch it. The sheep pushed in against his legs and he braced them, like being in a strong current, and held on to the bar of the trough. It was impossible that she was dead because his feelings for her had not diminished at all. It is the ability of a person to bring a reaction in us that gives us a relationship with them, and for the time they do that they have a livingness to them.

He remembered the sight of her in the cab of the tractor while she drove along the rows of bales and he stacked them on the trailer as the boys threw them up. He remembered the sweat and the itch of seed, the burn of the baling twine inside his fingers, the bales grazing his knuckles, the diesel air about the tractor. He remembered her with the bright splash of color of the cloth worn on her head, how they had joked that she looked girlish and Alpine. Heidi they had called her that day, and how he had wanted her in the rich way we can want a woman we physically work with, and how he was glad it was his wife he wanted this way.

How many reminders will there be? he asked. How many times will this happen to me? There is so much of her about. He was on the verge of anger, but then he had this sad, hopeless glow of warmth for her. I can hold on to her, he thought. I can hold on to her inside.

chapter two

THE BIG MAN drove off his place just before dark. In the back of the van he'd built a kind of keep with the straw bales and palettes and the badger was hidden amongst it. From the outside it looked like the van was filled with bales. The policeman had unnerved him and he could not shake the thought that they would come back as they had last time.

He had the six-month-old Staffy in for the ride. He needed a more stubborn dog and the Staffies were a good breed for that and were powerfully strong and he hoped to make a good tool of her to pull out the badgers and foxes. He thought about crossing the Staffy with something more mobile. Like Messie. He wanted to begin a breed of very sought-after and envied dogs.

He took it steady. The road was relatively easy, and he was pleased to be going south, the other carriageway filling and thickening with weekend traffic coming out to the second homes and caravans on the coast.

Two hours down the road he pulled into the lay-by they'd told him about and a while later another car pulled up.

It flashed its lights twice, turned in the lay-by and he followed. After a while, they turned off the main road.

The track seemed unnaturally wide for just a farm track and you could tell it had been tarmacked a long time ago and then it widened out further into a concrete road which met the yard. A number of cars were parked.

Where you would expect a farmhouse and outbuildings there was just yard and to one side a huge tin barn more like a hangar. You could see all this in the floodlights that lit the place off the big barn.

He got out of the van and could see two old buses to the side of the barn, their windows gone and the bonnets off and in the silver light that caught them there was something about them as of gutted big fish. He left the pup in the seat. He could see the faded paint of a sign that said Daycross Buses over the doors of the barn and understood the big parking yard now. The other guy got out of his jeep and came over and as he did there were the sounds of other men from the barn strangely muffled.

They opened the van and took out the palettes and then unbuilt the keep of straw.

He dragged out the badger in the sack and put it on the ground. He emphasized the effort.

Boar, he said. It's heavy.

The other man rolled the sack with his foot testing it and
the sack seemed to react shapelessly as if it were a col-
lapsed drunk. He had old army boots on. He was ratty
and bald and pinched and extruded, the opposite of the
big and gruff man. Let's take him in, he said.

There was a side door in the barn and they went through
that and there was an explosion of light and noise.
Around the walls were bales four or five deep to hold
the noise the way a big crowd would. In the center of
the depot was a mechanic's pit for working on the buses.
Around this the men had built stands to watch from.

The pit was lit with inspection lights and was a well of
brightness and the noise of the twenty or so men in there
was like before an amateur boxing match.

The door shut and some turned round and there were
cheers, seeing the sack. A dog barked as if it could scent
the badger.

At one end of the pit they had set up a trestle table and
the man behind it was obviously the boss. He had the
money tin in front of him.

The big man took the sack over and dumped it on the
table which shook the badger into life so it scuffed on

the table and rocked it. A can of beer went over to laughter as they held the table steady and then he punched the badger and it seemed to go still and there was a sense of immediate respect and dislike for him. It's a big, heavy boar, he said. Then they tipped the badger into the pit.

There were extra patches of black on the badger from the coal.

It fell awkwardly like a thing of weight and quickly righted itself and shuffled to each wall then backed itself into the corner in the blind light.

It lifted its head and scented the air, smelt the dogs that were setting off in the contagious excitement. The badger looked somehow unreal in the direct white light of the floods, its snout making little small circles. Any first bets? the man shouted.

A guy had come up and held a dog to the stand and the dog was frothing through its muzzle and was bright-eyed and you could see the movement of its heart quickly in its chest.

There were men leaning on the stands and weighing up the badger and some waiting to lay down bets until they'd seen a dog go in. Other men were bringing dogs around. Most were lurchers, but there were also other big dogs.

The badger moved in the pit and stood up on its hind legs against the wall like a bear and jogged about and tried to dig and the dogs frenzied and this seemed to transfer to the men. Then they put in a dog and it went at the badger.

The dog was a terrier and they put it in just to assess the badger before the big dogs started. He heard one man say that to another, and it was as if they were explaining it to him.

The terrier yapped and nipped and the badger put down its head into its front legs and relied on the thick hide and tough skin to take the nips and the men booed and hissed and the big man felt inside this anger at the badger and cursed him to fight.

A man hovered by with the tongs and prodded the badger as the dog darted in and the badger lifted and snapped back at the dog to a great cheer and the dog dived out of the way of the snap which had been like lightning.

The terrier bounced in and out at the badger, yelping and banging at him and trying to get in a nip and every now and then the badger uncoiled and snapped back to a great cheer. Then the badger stretched itself up and went at the dog with great ferocious energy and immediately caught the dog under the chin and tore open the side of the dog with its paw before the tongs smashed down on its neck and it let go of the dog which was whining and bleeding and dragging itself pathetically hurt around the floor of the pit. And there was a crazed sound from the men then.

First dog, called the man. Any bets?

The tongs had been welded for the job and were seven or eight feet long and they dragged out the badger and held it. While the bets went down they tore out its front claws. Then they held up its head and held its jaw open with a jemmy and smashed the front teeth. The badger was bloodied and struggling and the whole forty pounds of it trying to resist but the three or four men held it down while they did this and then they put it back in the pit.

The dogs were incensed now and in that deafening noise and light the big man looked down at the badger with a slow glee. One of the men had knelt on its back while they stretched out its legs and used the fencing pliers to tear out the claws and some of the claws had splintered and split rather than come free.

The man on its back had knelt hard on it while it struggled and grunted and humphed underneath him and he seemed to get something carnal and delicious from that. There was a steady buzz. There was a bloody smell in the room now.

He felt a well of company. The group's hungry cruelty seemed familial and safe to him and he felt for a moment his desires were not outlawed amongst them. He made their shouts internally, through his clenched teeth.

And then something changed. It came back at him.

The dogs were in cages at the far wall and the barred cages were in a row. People's skin under the brutal white light looked unnatural.

It was the gangness of it and the *group* of men and his outsideness of it; and he remembered the jail. There, staring into the pit, a brief dizziness came.

It's that police, he said. There was a holding to the way he talked to himself.

After an hour or so the men were drunk and baying as a pack. The badger could hardly fight anymore. Its chest heaved. It lay stupidly in the pit. A beer can was thrown in for encouragement, then another.

When finally it stirred, they put the dogs in again.

———

PART FOUR

The Sea

chapter one

———

DANIEL SAT IN the pickup in the car park looking out over the sea and he couldn't bring himself to open the door. He had meant to park in town but had driven through the sheer activity of cars and people with an alienated numbness and had gone on to the beach car park. The school was out on lunch and there were kids everywhere in the small town and it was all too much for him. He sat there staring out over the gray, heavy water.

He had realized that morning that there was no more toilet paper and could hardly believe that this would be the thing to drive him out.

People were walking their dogs along the seafront. They looked red faced, braced against the tide somehow with the gulls lifting and dropping over the water behind them. Cars were parked around him and people sat in them drinking from flasks and watching the waves, the windows misting with condensation, and it was visible to him the quiet companionship of the old couples there, their simple togetherness act of getting out of the house to go for a drive and watch the waves awhile. They seemed

to have the same comfortable look together as he had
felt with her in the shed when it rained. He felt the great
missingness of her then, watching the sea.

He'd had nothing substantial to eat for days. He was
becoming conscious of his cheeks, as if they were somehow
sucked in like they are in the cold, and there was a contin-
ual hollow sickness in his stomach. His teeth had begun
to hurt.

There was a much greater breeze here than inland,
and flecks of froth came off the waves into the wind.
He thought about walking into the waves until he dis-
appeared. It was the picture of himself old and alone.
He felt he would be about as substantial as those flecks.
When she asked him if he loved her, he had often said
and said sincerely that he could not imagine being old
without her. This was a constant, however tense things
got between them now and then. It seemed to be a sign
how much he knew of her that he could imagine her old
as well as he could recall her as a child, as if he could see
her at both ends of her life, see her completely. But he
could not imagine her dead.

He had shut the door of the bedroom. He understood
that at some point the scent of her would dissipate and go.

Beside him there was a boy in a car and he was looking
only at his phone and he could see the boy's face lit up
by the glow and not looking at the great, dramatic sea.

He wound down the window and turned on the engine and drove out of the car park to the garage on the outskirt of town.

He pulled the pickup over away from the fuel pumps and walked over the forecourt and into the garage and loaded his arms with the toilet roll he needed and took a four liter of milk from the fridge shelf. There was a truck driver there, pulling a coffee from the vending machine, but no one he knew.

He walked down the shelves and heard the truck driver go out and turned to watch and saw him bite into a hot roll as he left, briefly feeling hungry but pushing it down from habit, as if hunger was a memory rather than a call. Things on the shelves registered strangely to him, but each item seemed like it would demand something of him if he took it home: washing-up liquid, firelighters, a newspaper. Something urged him on to take these things and to get back to normality, but when he felt this swell of hope that the energy might be there for this, he reached out to touch it and it faded, and he just took the toilet roll and milk to the counter.

How are you keeping? said the garage owner. It was kind of balanced, how he asked it.

Yeah, said Daniel.

The garage owner nodded once. He totaled up the two items on the till.

You want me to book those? he asked. The two men had known each other a while now and they had only ever had conversations like this.

Daniel seemed momentarily confused at the question. Uh. Yes, he said.

Are you okay? asked the garage owner. He knew about his wife, like everyone. He didn't want to say anything too direct, but he liked the man. But he was trying not to show how he felt, seeing Daniel, which was the way you feel when you stop for an animal hit on the road.

Uh-huh, Daniel said. The garage owner looked at him, pushed his lips together in acceptance and nodded an o.k.

You want anything else? he asked.

No.

Anything to eat? There was a counter of hot food on display, cheese and ham pastries, a few pasties, some strips of bacon bedewed with fat under the hot light.

There was a brief flash of wide hunger but it was like he'd forgotten how to register it and Daniel said automatically:

No, I'm okay. The garage owner was looking at him as if he'd just seen him take a blow to the head.

Okay then.

Daniel took the goods from the counter and went out. He turned and nodded at the garage owner and went over the empty forecourt looking at the rich Georgian houses across the road.

He got into the pickup and was about to drive off when the garage owner banged the door and passed a wrapped bacon roll through the open window. His guts immediately roiled. He looked at the roll in this hands and the garage owner just banged the sill of the door and walked away.

———

Driving home he saw the badger on the road. He slowed. It was prone on the road. There was a magpie pulling at it. As he neared, the bird took a final pull and the leg raised as if it waved. Then it dropped again and the magpie let go of the scrap he was trying to loose, hopped, and went over the bank.

He did not understand. He had lived all his life here and he had never come close to hitting a badger.

He kept thinking of impact. Of horrible impact.

chapter two

HE SHIFTED THE bunched carrier bags and the cleaning stuff and the shoe polish and dustpan and brush and box of nuts and hinges and screws and found an empty jar under the sink and opened it and smelled it and it had no smell and he smelled only the lanolin and straw and always the undertone of cattle on his hands.

There had been a snatch of cold weather again that seemed to slow the lambing down for a while, and now there was only a handful of ewes left to lamb, and there was a reticence to them.

He had not yet accepted her death as a fact. It was impossible.

Daniel looked at the faded label stuck to the jar, peeled and lifted a little from being washed. Blackberry. He remembers the warm sun on his neck, the soft presence of her a few yards away, the firm pop of the pulled fruits.

He put the jar into his pocket and walked out through the back door and through the distraught garden and headed to the church, her piece of cloth crushed in his hand.

The church sat at the very top of the land, bordered with a wall and flanked on one side by dignified beeches. It was the church his mother and father were married in and the church where she was buried, right beside the land, as if she could stretch out in her sleep and feel it there. The day before her funeral, from the house, he had heard the slice of the spades digging the ground.

He knelt by the grave and took the jar and put in her piece of cloth inside its plastic bag and set the jar down for her, pushing it a little into the soft earth.

He cleared away the curled flowers and looked at the grave-marker. It looked plastic and new. It had no weight to it and no permanence. He read her name and put his hand in the dirt above her and he wanted to drag her from the earth again and have her there with him.

At the funeral he was in a daze, had the sure sense that she would be in the house when he returned there. He was at a distance from what was happening. There was the smell of opened soil like when they dug the garden together and he kept looking around for her. He had been driving once and two pigeons had come down on to the road and the car in front had failed to brake and hit one, mashing it to a paste with a dull thunk and brief change in speed. He felt the people look at him then with faces like the one he imagined he wore at that moment. Like they were aware he was about to be flattened by some terrible great thing.

> ...his days are like grass;
>   he flourishes like a flower of the
>   field;
> ...it is
>   gone,
>   and its place knows it no more.

He hears again the parson speak, words that chiseled into his brain like into the gravestone slate about him.

He refused that. I don't think it is true. He looked down at her and spoke as if to her. I don't think it's true. I think a place can remember.

He walked through the gravestones to the church gate and looked out over the sweeping valley. Red kites lifted above him, scanning over the bursts of gorse and he walked out of the church and followed the bridleway along the wall. He touched as was his way the ancient stones with their atlas of lichen mapped across them, looked down at the wasting piles of grass cuttings tipped from the mown churchyard, the scattered sprays of plastic flowers lifted from their places, broke vases and tattered ribbons from long-decayed bouquets, strange colors that were unnatural and minutely carnival there somehow. He hardly registered the van that passed. Did not look up. He was looking at the still-wet earth from the grave on his hands.

A place remembers, he thought. A place has to remember.

———

The big man saw Daniel there against the wall, clipped the verge briefly with his front wheel as he turned to look back at him. A thought came to him: The man was weak.

He watched the church recede in the mirror, slowed as he passed the farm lane, and let the thought fill out. He took the corner and pulled up upon the verge.

The big man was still uncomfortable. That policeman, he thought. Ag.

He'd taken the phone call that morning and there was not much time to decide things; the men were here tonight.

The first sett he had in mind was too close to outbuildings with men and dogs he did not know. This might be the place.

He's weak, the big man thought. He's weak and he is a farmer by himself. He will be occupied. News spread out here, soaked out, and he knew about the loss of Daniel's

wife and why he was at the graveyard. He's trying to get
through on his own.

He knew the setts locally and knew that this sett was relatively distant from the house of the farm. It was walkable
from his own place. It's the one, he said to himself. A
man on his own, what can he do?

He got from the van and it lifted and relaxed. In the fields
the lambs were bleating habitually and there was a green
bolt of new growth in the bank. He crossed the narrow
road and stood up into the hedge and looked over onto
the field. After the rain, the upper field was fizzing with
water. He studied it. He did not know if the badgers were
at the sett.

He got back in the van and drove a little way on then
parked by a gate and climbed over and cut back along
the top of the field. Then he followed the farm lane
down, and as he crossed over into a second field a rush
of thrushes came off the ground. He walked on, looking
at the bank.

Partway down the field there was a run in the bank. The
blackthorn that capped it was like a tunnel and the earth
was disturbed and excavated like a primitive road. There
were dropped piles of bracken by the run as if they had
been spilled.

He heard the gate clang the other side of the lane and then Daniel's weight land. He heard the bumps of footsteps approaching down the track.

He stayed very still.

When Daniel had passed, the big man looked at the gorse and at the thick-packed blackthorn and saw the stiff gray badger hair there.

That will do, he thought. He was decisive. That's enough of a sign.

He would take the risk that the badgers were there.

He knew the sett was in the woods at the far edge of the farm.

He'd have no reason to be down there, he said.

———

chapter three

WHEN DANIEL CAME into the shed the ewe looked immediately incorrect. She was stretched out, camel-prone in
the straw and her head was pushed out, the lips working
wildly, strained as if trying to get away from the pain at
the back of her body.

He swung over the hurdle into the pen of twins and went
to her. There were flecks of froth about her mouth as
she had been like this for some time, and he thought of
the sea and the waves, and of walking into them and the
hollow tiredness he felt.

The ewe was distended and her waters had broken but
there seemed to be too much thick blood and fluid in the
straw, as if it had sloughed out of her, and the other ewes
were unsettled and circled well away from her. He swore
over and over to himself, and this was his way of finding a
grip on things, of bringing it to a dealable realm.

He put his hand into the ewe and she bucked so he had
to lean on her and she glazed at him with crazy eyes as
she felt him stretch her and try to get his hand in to her
womb through the panicked muscles.

He found a head and with his thumb tried to follow its shape, to find the nose and the lobe of the skull and follow it back to the neck. He located a foreleg, bent over like an elbow, and drew it forward to lie against the neck like undoing a knot in the dark, feeling the extraordinary strength of the sheep's pelvis clamp on his arm.

The ewe panted and groaned and he closed his eyes and tried to see the shape of the lambs inside her with his hands. They are twins, he thought. They can often get crowded and bunched together and he gritted his teeth against the rejective, blunt, maw-like pressure of her pelvis as the ewe tried again to shift.

Something wasn't making sense. He did not understand and neither did the ewe. He tried to map the bodies inside her, followed a slick throat down to the forelegs, skimmed his fingers out to find a back knee. One lamb. He drew his arm out a little then found the second head, thinking it strange shaped at first, then understanding the soft bones above the eyes, found the flap of an ear and as he moved his hand he understood and the understanding rolled up in him like vomit.

The sheep was livid now in her pain and constantly noisome and he could feel her trying to expel the thing of pain in her, could feel the monstrous lamb being forced into the ungiving bones inside her.

When he stood up he felt sick and spots shifted in front of his eyes like motes of hay dust. Like the momentary surprise of picking up an empty box you thought was full of weight.

He went over to the kettle and looked for the knife and went in amongst the tools in the crate beside the gate. The vet would take too long. He was calculating this, trying to harden himself against his own want to not see anyone, to not have to talk and work with the vet. But he would take too long. I am not choosing this wrongly, he thought.

He poured boiling water over the knife and the hacksaw in primitive sterilization and went back to the ewe, tried to settle her. All her energy went on trying to expel the lamb and she was too exhausted to move and now and again butted her head into the block wall in distracted, impossible pain.

The ewe was slathered and he dried his hands and arms on the straw, wiping off the thick grease of fluid and blood and lubricant so that he could get more purchase on the saw and then with his left hand he reached in to the sheep and found the smaller, malformed head.

He was brutal now. A brutalness descended on him of necessity so that he may do this thing, and he drew out the mouselike head.

The sheep screamed and he pulled the head as far as he could, feeling back to where the stubbed neck married the one dead body inside. Then he pulled on the head in his hand to taughten that neck and cut into it with the hacksaw, the loose skin rucking under the blade until it scythed in and bit and sunk down through the hardly acknowledgeable flesh into the bastard spine.

He broke through the bone and the head lolled and he made taut the apron of meat and veins to go through them until the head came off.

As he let go, the stump went back into her body and the ewe tried to get up in shock and he had to weigh brutally on her while she bucked and kicked. There was blood all over her and there was blood in the straw and it flicked into his face and mouth as he held her until he felt the energy go out of her.

He went back into her and felt a sharp pain as she resisted, pushing the split vertebrae of the severed head into his knuckle. The ewe kicked him once, catching him below the knee, the force unbelievable but somehow lost in the noise of adrenaline and blood of them.

He put in his other hand and drew up the forelegs and gripped them in the vees of his fingers and he eased the other head through her opening, the dead body moving behind it, will-less and without life, like paste in a tube.

He got the head and feet out and went back and steered the sharp misgrown stump out of her then wrenched out the lamb.

The ewe lay gurgling and blinking, and even in this she turned in some maternal programming to clean her offspring and looked down on it, its hindquarters ungrown and fishlike, as if it grew strangely out of the pool of blood and fluids that messed the straw.

He looked at the lamb with a sick solid feeling and got up to get a sack.

When he came back with it, the ewe was licking the severed head and he felt sick well up in him. He tried to fight off the image of the destroyed head, of her destroyed head.

He gathered into the sack the lamb and the separate head and gathered up the filthy straw before he cleaned the saw and then his hands under the tap and took great desperate gulps of water. He poured iodine on his knuckles and bit his lip against the sting and sat down with his back against the standpipe. He was shaking, and from somewhere, a great hopeless anger began in him.

He wanted the final hit. He had just a little of something left in him to keep him going and he felt this great want for it to be knocked out of him, to suffer some unpassable collision so that he could just lie down. It was a kind of weak hopeless anger, and he felt calm now at the thought of failure. Like a boxer stumbling forward to welcome the punch that will put him finally down. Let him rest.

But God, he thought. There's this anger. It's the anger keeping me going. Gritting my teeth, pushing me on. It's like it is going to make me work it out, before I can stop.

She would not have liked that. She would not have liked this anger in me. I was not an angry man.

God, he thought, give me something to burn it out. He thought of a colossal car crash, of the huge finalizing impact. He put his palm against the upright and felt the rough wood there under his hand. The barn was full of her.

Then he thought of her with the cloth in her hair again. Of her smiling. I can do this, he thought. I can still do this. There was the huge responsibility of the farm and he would keep going because of it. He seemed to know though, that the need for the hit, the final crack, would come more and more.

chapter four

———

IT WAS BREWING to rain again, the sky bruising up and coming in from the sea.

The big man parked the van. All the rain had brought a sheen to the mud.

He got out and walked through the litter of tires and broken sheeting and the old scales of asbestos trod into the ground.

The dogs had started up at the sound of the van and he shouted them. They went quiet. There was the big mastiff in the shed, thumping with an animal weight against the wall.

The big man went in and made the call.

I've got the place, he said. He could not shake the thought of the policeman. It was like a tick in his brain. I'll leave the mastiff off, he thought.

•

The last time they had come they found the guns and
the illegal poisons and then the barks of the dogs they
brought with them settled to a low, locative yelp while the
officers photographed the finds in place.

When they searched further they found the money he
had accumulated but they did not notice his maps. They
found pornography and some old shooting magazines,
and they picked up the o.s. maps cursorily in the same
way as the pornography and the magazines and threw
them down again. His maps were his pride. They marked
every badger sett for miles around and though he had the
information in his mind, he had the special totemic asso-
ciation with the maps of the things we mark for purpose.
They somehow defined him.

The magistrate was a sleeping partner in a local construc-
tion firm and a member of the hunt and knew of the
man as a terrier man. There was a leniency. The things
they had found could be explained—the guns and poison
to keep down vermin; the undisclosed money from some
antisocietal feeling against bank accounts. The guns even,
in paranoia for the protection of this fund. He was defen-
sible like this, a forgotten outcast rejected by society just
trying to function his own way. But if they had linked up
the maps they might have begun to extrapolate, to trace
out the criminology of him.

When they took him, cuffed and bundled in the back of
a van, the place had the same vacated sense of a garden

after a storm. He was given a couple of months. He wouldn't get away with it again.

In his absence, his dogs had been put down.

———

Daniel looked down at the spent feed sack tied with baling twine lying at the foot of the stack, the mutilated lamb monstrous within it, its twin heads bagged together as if there was some conversation, some horrible severed dialogue. She didn't have to see that, he thought. She always hated that. Those terrible operations. Then he looked over to the gate where the tools lay, looked at the grotesque hacksaw.

He wondered what to do with the lamb and knew he would take it to the edge of the wood and just throw it there. He was supposed to declare it, do some paperwork, incinerate the carcass. But there was a pointlessness to that, and however unfarmerly it was to encourage them, he preferred that the dead lamb was taken by a fox, or buzzard perhaps. Perhaps the kites that scanned up the ground and wheeled always over the higher fields in the evening.

He put the sack in the bread crate at the front of the quad and cracked the bike on and went over the field. The gateway was soft and cut up and beneath him the pasture was spongy with the sitting water of weeks of rain.

He got off and swung open the bottom gate and sucked back through the mud to the bike and went through and down to the edge of the wood.

The field here was scrubby and drained into a small splash and as he dipped over on the bike a flight of teal went whistling into the air, crashing off the pond with the special vibrancy of smaller birds. He watched them go up at the extreme angle they took and wheel above the woods, piping and whistling with energy, before they cut away out of sight.

The teal were wild birds and followed the colder weather down as it crept south. When you held one, you understood how delicate and fine they were, and it was difficult to believe they could survive on the water.

This was the field where she had died. He looked back up to the farm, at the strange kelp of the tire tracks the bike had left in the wet fields and tried not to think of it.

He took the sack from the bike and undid the cord and tipped out the lamb. He shook the sack again and the severed head fell out and rolled a little like some grotesque ball. He had a moment of sickness, then he bent and picked up the loose head by the ear and threw it hard over the pond into the woods beyond.

He had the image of her lying there with a smashed head. His knees were in the wet ground and part of her face had gone like a crushed carrier bag and the blood leaked thickly in the surface water. He had heard the crack, had sensed it almost as something that shouldn't be in the panoply of sounds about the farm. It had been the speed of it. And then he had heard the horse run. There had been a split second as he registered the sounds, and then he had become this thing that just tried to get to her as fast as possible. She lived for five minutes maybe, that was it. She couldn't speak.

He sat down on the ground by the lamb. It started to rain again, the rain falling with a susurrating sound into the surface water of the field, almost hissing into the grass. There was the odd burst of water as a few stray teal returned into the pond.

The weight of the rain, the place he sat, some combination of things about him balled into another memory, of standing with the gun as they pushed the dogs through the woods. He could smell the foily metal of the gun, feel the rain soak into his hair and run down his skin, hear the snap of the rain on his waterproofs, waiting, focused and ready with a sense of strange timelessness, every now and then checking the position of the other guns waiting in the field. There was a shout of "over" and a cock pheasant came climbing out of the trees and he shot it as it accelerated, dropping it in the rushes that surrounded the pond. It was a direct and full shot and the bird had balled and fallen.

When they went to pick it up they couldn't find it. The bird had fallen like a stone and he had marked it, but when they went into the rushes they could not see it and the dogs were mad with the too-many scents that criss-crossed the space. They found a patch of feathers where there was impact, but the bird was gone and they wondered if something had been in the rushes and had been quick enough to take it unnoticed.

Three weeks later they were shooting again. He was on a hedge line and a cock came out running, one of the spaniels behind it. The dog got to it and mouthed it and he heard the handler call it off and shout to it to drop the bird and as he was the closest he jogged over to the bird and picked it up. It felt immediately thin and light, like an old person's hand, was not glorious in the way healthy wild things are.

He held the pheasant as the others came up and it looked at him and its eyes opened and closed once slowly, then it died. It just dropped dead in his hands. As it went limp he felt a mouthful of smell and when he looked at the bird and separated the feathers he saw that its back was grated with pellets and the gangrene had turned it a soft green. It was the bird he had shot, he was sure of that, and it had lived for three weeks like this, decaying, and it had died accusatorily in his hands. As if it was waiting for him, so that he saw. He kept seeing the way the eye had slowly opened and closed. It had taken the appetite to shoot away from him, and it was like a presentiment of something.

A few more teal came down in the splash. He felt distant. He felt distant from everything, the things inside him and the things around him.

Her death stayed at the same time incomprehensible and matter of fact, and he just sat there in the rain, getting colder and colder and listening to the susurrating sound of it hitting the surface water and wondering how deep her blood had gone.

———

PART FIVE

The Shard

chapter one

———

I'LL TAKE THE money first, said the big man.

It was close to Easter and the men wanted him to take them to a sett to work their dogs. They were Midlanders. They were mostly Midlanders or from the Valleys, the men that came to him for this, and it started mostly this time of year. It was a reason why you saw the number of dead badgers go up on the roads.

He folded the rolls of twenties and put them inside his coat and zipped it up.

We'll go down from here, he said. The men nodded. They were standing there with the two lurchers, one each on a lead, and the terriers were still in the car. The man had dumped a sack on the ground and the lurchers were looking intently at the sack. The men were wearing ex-army camouflage and it gave him an extra disgust of them.

At the presence of the new dogs the big mastiff was bridling in the shed and the shed walls thumped with the strength of him inside. Every now and then the men looked uncertainly over to the shed.

They got the tools together and rested them against the car. There were the spades and the long-handled pick. They had the iron spike and on the bonnet they laid out the billhook and the small axe and a short carpenter's saw.

The man came out of one of the sheds and put the snare wire on the bonnet and some pegs.

Likely won't be room for a pit, he said as he put the snares down. You want to do him out there? the man said, as if checking.

The men nodded. One of them, the skinnier one, already had this kind of cruel little firework going on in himself. The other man just looked like he liked to push things and break things and didn't look like he had the more sci-entific cruelness of the thinner man.

If you want to do him out there, there might not be room for a pit. If that's it, we'll put him on a tree.

The terriers inside the car were going crazy at the sight of the tools.

Gun?

The bigger man nodded and went to the car and brought back the shotgun in its case. He was physically unwieldy.

Licensed? asked the man and he nodded and said yes in the deep Birmingham accent. He had a neckless squareness but did not carry any look of great athletic power. It's a registered gun, he said, saying "gun" like it was the Welsh for it, with his accent.

They divided up the tools and got the terriers from the car.

What's in the sack? said the skinny one. It was like the bigger man had a caution and slowness in asking things and a respect for the other big man, but this skinnier one was more socially stupid.

He put down the sack again and drew out the fox. Without looking hard you would not have seen the burns in its eyes from it being frozen.

There were lambs bleating in the fields about and the light was just beginning.

We're after foxes, said the man. Clear? And the men nodded.

In the light the tools looked as if they were made of stone.

•

They walked down through the big man's land with the dogs and the tools, through the cemetery of machines.

The bigger man was an enthusiast of old cars and felt galled at the things he saw there, the Rover P6, the Triumph recognized only by its bones as if he was some adept mechanical archaeologist.

The men made no effort to cover their noise and as they passed the hedge they threw up the blackbirds that had sheltered here through the night and heard them batter into the remaining darkness with their laser-like call.

Messie went ahead and worked the bank but the other dogs were on leads, the lurchers livid with strain at the rabbits that went bumping away quickly from their torch-light. Here and there in the field were spent balloons of earthballs, their spores choked from them, like papery fruit.

They dropped down to a copse and went over the fence that marked the edge of his land, heard the small breeze amplify in the hazel around them. There was no true need for the torches but the townsmen were not used to such darkness nor this level of quietness and they were not restful in it.

•

When they came out of the copse the big man told them to turn off the torches and for moments they were blind. Then shapes came out, like shapes on a wax rubbing as their eyes adjusted.

There was a low open field to cross.

Are they broken to stock? asked the man.

Both the men nodded.

We can't have them going for the stock.

The men looked into the field and eventually made out the strange bulks of cattle. The men were nervous at the cattle. They were neither used to big animals.

Farm buildings were beyond the field and the lights from the house looked to be guttering through the naked trees that were before it.

They went over the fence and followed the hedge line out of the field and went away on to the upper fields and out onto a road. Then they cut off the road on to a bridle path. There were houses in sight and they did not use the torches and slipped and cursed on the path, following mostly the pull of the dogs. The bigger man was heaving and panting and his asthma was getting up. Every now and then you could hear the hiss of him as he used the inhaler and it looked childlike, a big man like that using such a small thing. It made him look like a simpleton.

There was a luminous blue light come now and they stopped awhile and looked out over the valley, the strange puffs of sheep coming visible, the whitewashed farm-houses with their twinkling windows quartz-like in the flat gray land.

Some birds were now up, and strangely in that light a group of gulls went ghostly off toward the beach, as if fleeing the coming light. You could not see the sea from here, but there was the sense of it.

They looked out across the feminine curves of the hills and the man told them where they would go. Then they cut along the church wall, the dogs sniffing at the magpie-lifted ribbons and plastic flowers that had come over from the graveyard, and they went over the fence and into the sloping field.

The big man knew that up here they could not be seen from the farm.

Those are the woods, he said. He pointed. There was the dark mass, like hair on a body, straight before them. We'll work our way about to it, he said. The farm is just down there. They could hear the muffled sounds from the barn.

The lurchers were stiff at the sheep, and the ewes brayed and stamped the ground.

It's not easy land, he said. There's some boggy stuff to work through. He was thinking of the man with the asthma, not with concern but with a sort of despisement.

The terriers were stiff and shaking already with excitement.

Take the gun out, he said. Give me the dogs.

The bigger man unsheathed the gun and broke it and held it in his arm and the other big man took the dogs.

Now, he said. Go.

The men worked their way across the fields, staying well up on the hedge lines out of eyesight from the farm. They came in to the pond field from the side and hurried the exposed few yards into the woods. The settled ducks set to chucking and gawping on the water but they did not lift into the unpredictable light.

Once inside the woods, the big man knew it was safe to use the torches carefully again.

Keep them to the ground, he said. If you shine them up he'll see them.

———

The owl cut low against the bracken and its wings tilted and it stretched out its furred legs in a way that was somehow catlike and landed on the post and its white also was the very clean white of a cat that has white to it. Then it saw Daniel, and went off over the scrub, leaving the strange white silent thing of itself, like snow can.

He had been unable to sleep. He had come to believe that things had gone wrong because of the shard. That its removal had somehow upset a balance.

He had lain thinking of the vertebral spike of the malformed lamb, and that had brought him to this thought.

He stood over the shard. He had given it animation and it still had some presence to him but it was like a dead animal there.

He stood in the field. There was severity, a strange squareness. The cuts of hazel still stood out.

The ground was beginning to burst with growth now. The thin spears of grass looked fabricated, too fine and too green against the clay. Every here and there came a compact nettle. There was a part light. In the places where the water still stood the ground hissed, but much of the rain had run off into the new blatant ditches.

He went to the near fire pile and kicked a little at the crust of ash. It had turned a gray pink now, still with a white powder from the passing of great heat.

He dragged the long branch from the pile and walked from the fire until it was free and then weighed on it so it snapped where the flames had burnt and thinned it. There was a burst of charcoal, a blackbird, a sudden quick call in the quiet.

Daniel kicked at the burnt end he had formed and rolled it to make the hard point of a thick spear. Then he went to the cut that the shard had come from. The earth had hardened with time, healed somehow. It was a scar.

He used the pole spade-like to push back in some earth and kicked and scuffed at the bent lip of soil. Again he thought: Why do I not bring the things I need with me? As she would have done. He thought of the owl. It had been around more now. He could not separate it from her.

With the empty tub of a discarded salt lick he went back and forth from the fireplaces and filled the hole with wet ash and again kicked at the soil and mud. Then he used the pole like a spike and began to remake the hole. A cold sweat started on him, as if there was a coldness even to his energy now, no extra heat.

•

For a few feet or so it skidded on the wet ground but then the shard bit and he raised it up. He felt the familiarity of it, under his hands.

He found hold and walked it patiently to the hole, lifting it and dropping it, lifting it and dropping it. Then he bear-hugged the shard, and with all the strength he had raised it and let it go. It planted itself with its own weight.

He stood and looked once briefly for the owl, believing somehow it might be there.

For a moment he believed he heard voices, but he dismissed it.

He looked at the shard. It was taller than him, this way.

I'll bring the tractor, he thought, knock it in with the front loader. He felt he must restore something.

Then he saw for the first time the marks in the iron, a strange part-familiar lettering, a strange ogham there below where it would have been in the ground.

He could not explain it, but he felt that there would be a rightness now. That it should never have been moved.

chapter two

———

THE BIG MAN assessed the space. The mound seemed to be set in some old clearing. It was ringed with thicker, older trees. There was a hollow before it as if the mound had been formed by some great digging out at some point. For some reason the man thought of the cell. It was perhaps the thick wall of trees.

That policeman, he thought. He could not stop thinking of the four walls, the hatch for food, the dog-pen proximity of others. It was the worst thing for him: to be surrounded by people and to be forced to fit in the social system of them. He was too much an instrument to change what he did, but he had a strange feeling of exposure now. He was nervous about the policeman. I can't go back, he said to himself. I wouldn't get away with it again.

He took a lantern and lit it on the ground to keep the light low. The man could see the mound was heavy with holly and it had a freshly washed look of newness in that light.

Ag, I should get rid of the gun, he thought. Nothing else is so serious. They won't catch me for anything else.

141

Thinking of the things he did, his mind whetted at the thought of the badger.

Take the dogs and find the holes, said the big man. Leave the lurchers. When you find a hole, cut some holly and stuff the hole with it, then close it up with stones. Or dead wood. Make it heavy. Keep the dogs to hand for now.

We've dug before, said the skinny man. The big man just looked at him as if he could ball him up like paper.

When the town men came back they took a drink then went to the entrance hole with one of the dogs. The big man was holding the spade and it had the look of a cudgel in his hands.

They fixed the locator to the dog and sent it in.

The skinny man began to work his way over the mound, staring at the locator. The big man spat thickly. He remembered the sound of the dogs at the bus depot. Then the dog began to yelp.

The big man eddied on the sound. He was trying to picture the system of the sett.

They followed the locator until it pinpointed the dog. There was an excitement amongst the other two men.

The big man staved his spade into the ground. Here, he said. Dig here.

———

chapter three

ABOUT AN HOUR had gone by and there had been a brief
fall of rain. They worked in the lantern light and everything beyond the space it lit looked impenetrable and
dark. At the edge of the wood a robin was singing, undis-
turbed by the digging within, and there was something
unsettling in that.

They had left the other dogs off the mound in the clearing
and they were variously slumbered or cleaning themselves
when the fox came through them. The fox seemed to be
in their midst before it understood and the dogs exploded.

The men were straight off the mound to the dogs but the
noise had been massive and abrupt. The fox had gone,
and they couldn't understand how a fox could come into
the smells of them and the sound of them digging but
it had and the dogs' reaction had shattered through the
cloak of trees.

•

Daniel was going through the cattle when he heard it. He stopped. For a moment he listened to the rattle of the corrugated iron as one of the cows scratched inside the barn, and to a tractor clanging as it changed loaders on the next farm.

His own dog was up and alert on the roof of the kennel and there was the clink of its chain as it scented the air, smelling the echo of sound. Over the cwm the sound had set other farm dogs off but he knew what he had heard. It was not fox, he was sure. The bark was different from the sheepdogs. Smaller dogs.

He stayed still, as if recalling the sound, trying to pin it down, and then went through the cowshed and looked out over the dark fields to the woods. Sounds came to him through a wall of thought. He listened hard.

The men settled the dogs and when the sheepdogs in the nearby farms started up they saw it could cover the thing.

The big man was looking at the tops of the trees for the breeze to see which way the sound might have gone. He listened for the sound of a quad bike. When there was none after some time he seemed to settle. He had been like an animal growing in its senses and his whole frame in the big coat seemed to shrink minutely as he relaxed.

He could hear faintly the echoey sound of the sheep in the barn above and thought the noise inside must be complete and heavy. Ag, he thought. You wouldn't hear it over that.

After a while they started again to dig.

Daniel stayed still, listened. He had just fed the sheep and they were only just quietening from the great bleating they made as he unfolded the hay. They had fallen quiet with eating now, and he listened. The dogs had bothered him. It was trancelike, like feeling for a lamb, as if his mind felt round his land like a great hand feeling for something wrong, some fault in its body, some small thing out of place.

And then he heard it, was sure he could hear it. Some tap foreign to the concert of the land. Once. Twice maybe. It wasn't a random sound; it was a sound of work. A tink far away, like the sound of a thrush cracking a snail. And then it was gone again.

Despite the cold the skinny man worked in his T-shirt and you could see the national tattoo turn grotesque with the work and the strange, febrile bulldog inside his forearm.

147

He had the peculiar heating of fatless men and he swung the pick onto the stone a second time before the man could stop him, and then a third, shattering the thick leaf of shale, the strange percussive noises going off into the air.

Too much noise, said the big man. Next time dig round.

He had this strong captaining and the skinny man looked at him guiltily. It was like he was drunk in the effort and he was showing a kind of childlike excitement. The big man just stared right through him. Then he went off into the woods.

Daniel went into the house and through the kitchen and went into the lean-to for the gun.

He opened the cabinet and took out the .410. Then he put it back and took out the twelve bore.

In his tiredness the gun felt heavier than he remembered. He breached it. The smell and the look of the gun made him think of the shard, the metal smell still somewhere on his hands.

He took a box of cartridges and went through again to the kitchen. Then he got the bag of rice and prepared to swap the lead out of the cartridges.

The Aga pinged and drew his attention and he put the gun down breached on the table and took the box from the open oven.

The lamb was dead. It was dead and comfortable.

He put his hand to the lamb's ribs. Nothing.

He got up and put the gun back in the cabinet, and then went out. And there was something sacrificial in the way he did.

———

The skinny man was in the hole passing the dirt up to the asthmatic man. It was deeper than him, and you couldn't see the skinny man unless you looked right in.

Every now and then the big man passed water down to him which he tipped on his head as if he were too hot. They were close to the badger now and they could sense this closeness and the men talked encouragingly to the dog.

The big man had returned and was standing with the dogs.

This is it, thought Daniel. This is the last bit I have. Right here. He was down on the wet ground clenching his fists and trying to calm himself and rouse himself all at once. He could feel his fists sink into the wet earth.

He listened to the men call to the dog, could hear the accents, hear the spade slice the ground, muffled, the men digging her grave at a distance. The noise of the work and the slope of the mound protected him and he looked up through the big trees, then down at the place around the dig.

There was a pile of severed roots. The tools.

He felt something set in. This is it, he said to himself. He could smell the new opened ground. Then he stood up, and the dogs went berserk.

The spade coming was like the wing of a bird.

He watched the jay pick up from the ground the leftover food they always threw from the door. He watched the day sink. The cold snap had come, the low sun started to decline.

He was looking at the jay. They had grown more confident now, since more magpies had been trapped in the hedgerows, like they filled their space. The jay was curious moving and the same color as the sunset and he was looking at the symmetry of that color and thinking of the pink cloth she had lost.

He heard the door click and the jay startled and flew off, the blue splash of its wings dazzling in their selfness against the bird.

She came out, pushing her feet into her boots. She looked bigger than she really was in her clothes. From the house came the smell of warm bread.

I'm going down to the horse, she said.

He watched her walk away. The light seemed to vibrate in the land and he felt a great love for it, as if he had seen it anew. He had the great, choking feeling.

The sun was dropping before her and he watched her go over the fields.

This is everything. This is everything I need, he said.

———

epilogue

They pull up the cars some way off from the place and get out, holding the latches up as they push the doors to. It is impossible to be silent with the wet ground. The dogs pant, scuffle.

The policeman looks down at the wet ground while the others get out around him, get readied. He presses his foot into the mud of the verge, lifts it deliberately. When he checks his torch, his footprint is clear and defined. He thinks of the earth of the sett, its witness. There are the boot prints. Matches of soil. A dog's hair taken from the mouth of a tunnel.

There is the faintest squelch on his radio and he presses his ear, nods there in the darkness. The teams are in place. The greatest risk is the dogs.

Perhaps in his sleep the big man distantly registers the clink of chains, the click of doors, the suck of footsteps. As if they happen in some earth some way above him. Then they come, with an immediate noise.

He is sleeping and stunned bright light-like for a moment
into a childlike immobility. His own dogs echo riot in the
sheds and the police dogs respond, deafening in the low,
crouched house. And though this is his space he is disori-
ented, startled and slow.

In the confined room the constant yelps are deafening
and confusing and like bright lights to the man, and he is
unsure what he can do.

Lights blind his eyes, a dog barks inches from his face.
There is nowhere to go. He has nowhere to go.

In the small hole of his room he feels sick misunder-
standing fear and lashes at the dog, kicks and scuffs as he
cowers, finds himself stopped up against the wall, tries to
use the thick blanket like a hide.

The handler shouts him to be still, to stay still in the spat-
tering space of noise, the sniffer dogs breathing through
the tunnels of the house, the shouting men.

He sees past the dog's glaring eyes the metal cuffs, the
instruments readied for his taking. He revolts again but the
dog yaps. The dog yaps. The dog yaps every time he moves.

acknowledgments

Thanks to the Society of Authors for a Foundation Award and to Literature Wales for a bursary, both of which gave me time with the book.

Thanks to Gordon Lumby of Badger Watch & Rescue Dyfed for confirming things I already knew, and for furnishing me with details I didn't.

To John Freeman and Philip Gwyn Jones, for consecutive votes of faith.

Thanks too, Jon McG., Euan, and Ch. and the rest of you. You know who you are.

Also by Cynan Jones

The Long Dry

Everything I Found on the Beach

FORTHCOMING FROM COFFEE HOUSE PRESS IN 2016

from

The Long Dry

the Cow

He'd woken earlier and gone out to check the cows. The night had been still and again he could not sleep with all the thoughts filling the silence of the unmoving night; so he had got up and gone into the clear, still morning. For very long it had been very still. It was before the light came up.

With the light of the torch he found the stillborn calf dead in the straw of the barn. He rubbed the stump of his missing finger. He could see the cows' breath in the morning air—which even then was cold—and a warm steam off some of their bodies. The mother of the stillborn calf was kneeling beside the calf lowing sadly and gently. The other animals hissed and puffed and chewed straw.

He took the dead calf by its ankles and lifted it from the straw that was bloodied by birth, not by the calf's death. It was strange because the mother had licked the calf clean. He thought of the mother cow licking her calf and not understanding why it would not stand clumsily to its feet, its legs out of proportion, its eyes wide. Why the incredible tottering new life of it did not come.

161

He carried the calf out of the barn, counting the cows inside, and went out into the field. Kate would be sad about the calf. The calves died very rarely for them.

Over the hills behind the farm the light started. Just a thinning of the very black night that made the stars twinkle more, vibrate like a bird's throat and put out a light loud compared with their tininess. He'd noticed the missing cow.

He'd hoped it had got out of the barn and into the field, where there were other cows with older calves out. She was very close to calf and heavy and perhaps went because of the terrible thing of the stillbirth.

In the dark he could not see the cow and he carried the dead calf across the field, hard grazed because there had been no rain. Somewhere, a large truck growled along the road, near the land he had his eye on. He dropped the calf into the old well at the bottom of the field because he did not want Kate to see it and because it was expensive to send in the dead calves to find out why they died. You always lose some, he knew. There is no reason. You will just lose some. He hoped the cow had not gone missing.

the Farm

The farm sits on a low slope a few miles inland from the sea. Gareth's father bought the farm after the war because he didn't want to work for the bank any more. The farm had belonged to an eccentric old lady who was found feeding chickens in her pajamas by the postman one morning. She had no chickens. Three sons and her husband had gone to war and they were all killed in the war one after the other, in order of age. When they found her feeding chickens that were not there she was taken away and put into a home where she died of a huge stroke like she couldn't be away from the farm. When Gareth's father bought it, the farm was collapsing.

The family moved in with the intention of rebuilding, of refurbishing the farm; but after the first few frantic months they did little and settled into the place. Things took on names—the rooms and the fields.

In the new house, after the floors were redone and the walls sealed and plastered, painted brightly, things were placed here or there—the ornaments and bowls. It was too deliberate, like posing for a photograph, and odd to Gareth, who was young then.

When the house started to live around its new people, things seemed to find a more comfortable place for themselves—like earth settling—haphazard and somehow right, like the mixture of things in a hedge. They relaxed and walked round the house in their shoes. Before that, for a while, it had seemed to the children like the house was bewildered by the attention—it was like they were when their mother wiped their face with a cloth.

———

"I wanted him last night," she thinks. "Really. And then I don't know. It went away again. I went flat, like I was numb, when he started touching me, and I tried to be patient and coaxing but he could tell, so he stopped and he didn't say anything. I could tell he was angry. Not really with me, just, he's been very good recently not starting anything and then I started something. And then he knew I didn't want it; and I don't know why. I miss his hands. God, I miss his hands."

She's started this, now. This way of thinking—as if she's talking aloud with herself, as if she is a face framed in a mirror talking back to her. A means of control, or of measure. Of trying to make sense. Women get old quickly, when they get old.

She feels her body moving under the rough cloth of his shirt, which she has thrown on to be out of bed. In the mirror, behind her, the unmade bed. She feels her body is soft and filled with water and dropping with age, and there is no way he can look at her now and feel the things he has felt for her in the past. He will want her because of his care for her now, not out of desire. It's like being allowed to win a game. He can't possibly want her body. She wonders about cutting her hair short again.

———

Sometimes they go funny. When they're fat with calf. They go funny and they do something, and it's impossible to guess what they have done by trying to think like them. Because they don't think when they do this. If they decide to go they can go a great distance. Just stumbling and crashing along and it doesn't make any sense. All you can do is try and find them and hope they are okay and do what you can. Stay near them. Check them. Mostly they're okay once the calf has come.

———

Everything I Found on the Beach

The sergeant was on the beach and looked down at the body and the younger policeman Morgan was with him and it was the first time for him, seeing something so severe.

The body had most of the fingers of one hand off and there was a big wound to the face and out through the back of the head.

The tide had lapped up on the body and the salt water had swelled the edges of the big wound. It was early but the birds had been awake and the eyes were already gone. It was really severe to look at.

The owlish man got out of the taxi that he'd just rolled up along the little slip to the beach and came down the slip and called out to the young policeman.

The sergeant looked up tiredly. "Christ," said the sergeant. "Keep him away."

The young policeman saw a small crab scuttle from under the face of the body and it seemed to dislodge the balance of the head so it rolled slightly, as if it moved in its sleep. It made the young policeman feel sick. "What have you got, Morgan?"

The young policeman went up to the owlish man who was standing by the blue and white tape the other police had put up. The owlish man was pecky and curious looking.

167

"What have you got?" he asked again.

Morgan shrugged. "We don't know yet. We're not sure." He looked very pale and sick.

The sand beach was long and slightly curved and the water hissed where the edge of the tide petered out. They were putting up a screen now around the body and the owlish man was looking, trying to see whatever he could.

"When did you find him?" asked the owlish man.

"Right early. Someone walking a dog."

The old guy had been walking his dog and described how the dog had run up to the corpse and scattered the birds and the idea of the birds pecking at the face made Morgan sick inside again.

"You look paler than when I picked you up the other night," said the owlish taxi driver, trying to be light.

The owlish man could just see the legs of the body now. The legs looked distraught and wet like the tide had been over them and he noticed the kind of shapeless deadness to them as if they weren't real.

"Any explanation? Nothing on him?" asked the man.

"No." The policeman had swallowed down his sickness once more. "No. Unless the tide took it. He could have been washed up. We're not sure yet."

"Didn't happen here then?"

"We don't know," said the policeman. He thought about the fingers missing and about the big wound to the face. He wanted to go back to the body. It was easier actually being by it and looking at it like a big fact. There was something unreal and factual and more dead about the body that way and it was easier to deal with.

The sergeant called up to the young policeman.

"I shouldn't be talking to you," Morgan said to the owlish man. He got more formal. "I can't give you any information at the present time. I'll have to ask you to leave the scene."

Other men had parked up and were coming down the slipway in white forensics suits onto the beach. There was something weird about the beach that looked like it had been busier at one time, some time in the distant past. But then it had been abandoned, fallen out of favor.

"You don't know who it is then?" asked the owlish man.

The young policeman had turned to go back.

"No." He had the thought of the gulls pulling at the dead face. "We've got no idea who it is yet."

COFFEE HOUSE PRESS

THE MISSION OF COFFEE HOUSE PRESS is to publish exciting, vital, and enduring authors of our time; to delight and inspire readers; to contribute to the cultural life of our community; and to enrich our literary heritage. By building on the best traditions of publishing and the book arts, we produce books that celebrate imagination, innovation in the craft of writing, and the many authentic voices of the American experience.

Visit us at coffeehousepress.org.

FUNDER ACKNOWLEDGMENTS

COFFEE HOUSE PRESS is an independent, nonprofit literary publisher. All of our books, including the one in your hands, are made possible through the generous support of grants and donations from corporate giving programs, state and federal support, family foundations, and the many individuals that believe in the transformational power of literature. We receive major operating support from Amazon, the Bush Foundation, the McKnight Foundation, the National Endowment for the Arts—a federal agency, and Target. This activity is made possible by the voters of Minnesota through a Minnesota State Arts Board Operating Support grant, thanks to a legislative appropriation from the arts and cultural heritage fund.

Coffee House Press receives additional support from many anonymous donors; the Alexander Family Fund; the Archer Bondarenko Munificence Fund; the Elmer L. & Eleanor J. Andersen Foundation; the David & Mary Anderson Family Foundation; the W. and R. Bernheimer Family Foundation; the E. Thomas Binger and Rebecca Rand Fund of the Minneapolis Foundation; the Patrick and Aimee Butler Family Foundation; the Buuck Family Foundation; the Carolyn Foundation; Dorsey & Whitney Foundation; Fredrikson & Byron, P.A.; the Jerome Foundation; the Lenfestey Family Foundation; the Mead Witter Foundation; the Nash Foundation; the Rehael Fund of the Minneapolis Foundation; the Schwab

Charitable Fund; Schwegman, Lundberg & Woessner, P.A.; Penguin Group; the Private Client Reserve of US Bank; VSA Minnesota for the Metropolitan Regional Arts Council; the Archie D. & Bertha H. Walker Foundation; the Wells Fargo Foundation of Minnesota; and the Woessner Freeman Family Foundation.

ALLAN KORNBLUM, 1949–2014

Vision is about looking at the world and seeing not what it is, but what it could be. Allan Kornblum's leadership and vision created Coffee House Press. To celebrate his legacy, every book we publish in 2015 will be in his memory.

THE PUBLISHER'S CIRCLE
OF COFFEE HOUSE PRESS

PUBLISHER'S CIRCLE MEMBERS make significant contributions to Coffee House Press's annual giving campaign. Understanding that a strong financial base is necessary for the press to meet the challenges and opportunities that arise each year, this group plays a crucial part in the success of our mission.

"Coffee House Press believes that American literature should be as diverse as America itself. Known for consistently championing authors whose work challenges cultural and aesthetic norms, we believe their books deserve space in the marketplace of ideas. Publishing literature has never been an easy business, and publishing literature that truly takes risks is a cause we believe is worthy of significant support. We ask you to join us today in helping to ensure the future of Coffee House Press."

—The Publisher's Circle Members of Coffee House Press

PUBLISHER'S CIRCLE MEMBERS INCLUDE
Many Anonymous Donors
Mr. & Mrs. Rand L. Alexander
Suzanne Allen
Patricia Beithon
Bill Berkson & Connie Lewallen
Robert & Gail Buuck
Claire Casey
Louise Copeland
Jane Dalrymple-Hollo

Mary Ebert & Paul Stembler
Chris Fischbach & Katie Dublinski
Katharine Freeman
Sally French
Jocelyn Hale & Glenn Miller
Roger Hale & Nor Hall
Jeffrey Hom
Kenneth & Susan Kahn
Kenneth Koch Literary Estate
Stephen & Isabel Keating
Allan & Cinda Kornblum
Leslie Larson Maheras
Jim & Susan Lenfestey
Sarah Lutman
Carol & Aaron Mack
George Mack
Joshua Mack
Gillian McCain
Mary & Malcolm McDermid
Sjur Midness & Briar Andresen
Peter Nelson & Jennifer Swenson
E. Thomas Binger and Rebecca Rand Fund
of the Minneapolis Foundation
Jeffrey Sugerman & Sarah Schultz
Nan Swid
Patricia Tilton
Stu Wilson & Melissa Barker
Warren Woessner & Iris Freeman
Margaret & Angus Wurtele

For more information about the Publisher's Circle and other
ways to support Coffee House Press books, authors, and activi-
ties, please visit www.coffeehousepress.org/support or contact
us at: info@coffeehousepress.org.

CYNAN JONES was born near Aberaeron, Wales, in 1975. He is the author of three novels, *The Long Dry* (winner of a Betty Trask Award, 2007), *Everything I Found on the Beach* (2011), and *The Dig* (2014), winner of the Jerwood Fiction Uncovered Prize. He is also the author of *Bird, Blood, Snow* (2012), the retelling of a medieval Welsh myth. *The Dig* is his first novel published in the U.S.